SUSANNA'S MIDNIGHT RIDE

The Girl Who Won the Revolutionary War

LIBBY CARTY MCNAMEE

SAGEBRUSH
PUBLISHING

For Bernie, My Dearest Friend

Remember the Ladies, and be more generous and favorable to them than your ancestors. Do not put such unlimited power into the hands of the Husbands.

— ABIGAIL ADAMS TO JOHN ADAMS

CONTENTS

SUSANNA'S MIDNIGHT RIDE

CHAPTER 1
DEAD OR ALIVE?

Tomorrow I'll find out if my brothers are dead. A new casualty list is due over at the trading station in Petersburg. Dread seeps through my body like a poison as terrifying scenarios flash through my mind. I must keep these fears to myself, or at least hidden from Mother. She's my namesake, Susanna Bolling, but I didn't inherit her strength. She shows no tolerance for weakness, but deep down even she must feel it, too. How could she not? After all, Stith and Alexander are both her sons. They've been off fighting for American liberty, and the last five years have felt like centuries. To this day, Mother insists their beds remain freshly made here at Bollingbrook Plantation, ready for them to return at any minute.

For the last few days, April showers have soaked our tiny village of City Point, Virginia, washing away the sticky layer of yellowish-green pollen. Much to my dismay, this has inspired Mother to come up with a wearisome list of chores. Fresh green shoots are covering our sprawling fields, but I can't appreciate this new life. My nerves are far too raw. I can safely say that no one expected the war to last this long, certainly not the ogre known as King George. Instead of getting easier, though, waiting for news has only become more trying. Constant worry sapped my limited patience long ago.

The brutal British continue to try to bully us into submission, but the war feels a world away here at sleepy Bollingbrook. It's no wonder. After all, I'm currently sweeping up the dust balls scattered across my bedroom, a tedious task. As much as I fear for my brothers' safety, I must confess something. I'm a bit jealous. If I have to endure this ghastly war, how I long to participate. Yet I cannot, for one simple reason. I'm a girl. So here I remain, trapped, wielding a broom instead of my own Brown Bess musket and bayonet.

I still remember watching through a lens of tears as my brothers swaggered down the lane, having insisted on walking to enlist in our Virginia militia. Full of cocky smiles, they sauntered off to the courthouse, chattering about liberty, no taxation without representation, and honoring dear Father's memory. At first Stith wrote often, full of determination and hope, but his letters dwindled, seemingly along with his confidence. We haven't received word since Christmas. Mother and I avoid the subject altogether, refusing to acknowledge the dark fears we can't help but harbor. I pray tomorrow's list won't explain this deafening silence and make it permanent.

Reluctantly, I force myself to keep sweeping, but housecleaning has never felt so meaningless. My broom catches on something behind the quilt stand, but I'm lost in my turbulent thoughts and ignore it. Finally I relent, and kneel down with a sigh to peer between the twigs. There lies a blue clay marble from a game Stith and I played years ago. Despite the layer of sweat covering my body, the sweet memory sends a shiver down my spine.

I look over at my house servant, who is engrossed in untangling my gowns and hanging them on wall pegs. Despite my good intentions, my frustration bubbles over. "Penny, I can't stand waiting another minute! I'd give anything to stop my mind from racing."

Her dark face breaks into a sad smile. "Miss Sukey, all that worrying of yours ain't helping them none. You got to keep strong." She shakes her head. "That's all you can do."

Born within months of each other, Penny and I have been raised together for sixteen years. Our stations couldn't be any more different, but I can't imagine life without her by my side.

I walk over to the window and stare through its wavy glass. "How I'd love for the boys to come traipsing over that hill right now, bragging about licking those awful Redcoats." I let out a raspy sigh. "But that's impossible, not with our cause hanging by a thread. And there's not a thing I can do to change it."

Penny shakes her head. "But at least you safe here at Bollingbrook. Like your mama say, war ain't no place for a lady."

I bristle. But before I can respond, a rapid movement outside catches my eye. I open the window and lean out. My eyes widen. Oh, no! It's Mother, stalking over to the towering oak tree. Her fists are clenched and her back is ramrod straight. Penny's younger brother Leroy is trailing along behind her. My heart sinks. What in the world has happened? He was just hauling water up from the river, like he does every day. I frown. I bet Mother caught him fishing with the buckets again. Hopefully he's not telling her another tall tale. Sometimes that boy doesn't know when to stop chattering.

I steal a glance over at Penny. Thankfully she's swiping at cobwebs and humming "Yankee Doodle" so I don't breathe a word. She worries about Leroy too much as it is.

Wiping sweat from my brow, I break into a rant to keep us both distracted. "No matter how many times we clean this house, it doesn't mean anything." Even though Mother is quite occupied outside, I still keep my voice low, given my quarrelsome tone. "It won't make the boys any safer or turn the tide of this godforsaken war."

"They be fine." Penny thumps her chest. "I feel it right here."

If only I shared her confidence. But no matter how hard I try, I can't find any reason for such optimism. Thankfully, Fate has spared us for the last five years. But surely our luck will run out soon, just like the Continental Army's ammunition supply.

Overcome by my woes, I groan, "It's all so unfair, and this heat is driving me mad. We wouldn't be nearly so hot if we could wear trousers like the boys." I shake my head. "I suspect this spring cleaning is just Mother's way to busy us until tomorrow."

Now dusting at a furious pace, Penny darts around the room. Every inch of her body is in motion. Even the feather duster is an extension of her calloused fingers. "Right easy for me to say, I know. Leroy be here safe, even if he nothing but trouble nowadays." She shrugs and shakes her head. "He ain't the same brother I knew." My heart melts for her. Naturally her loyalties are divided. He's still her little brother after all.

The thought of Leroy unnerves me, so I try to avoid the topic altogether. But for the past few weeks, I've agonized over his situation. I can't decide whether Mother was right to accuse him of stealing her favorite brooch. To make matters worse, it was Father's last Christmas gift to her before he passed away. But who else could've taken it? Leroy was the only other person in her bedroom that day. Then again, he'd been her chore boy for years without incident, other than fresh loaves of bread disappearing from the cookhouse. For such a skinny boy, he sure can eat. I can still see the tears streaming down his face and dripping from his trembling chin as Mother peppered him with questions.

I shake my head.

Mother ordered several searches of the slave cabins, but to no avail. To her credit, she finally dropped the matter, but remained suspicious. I still don't know what to think. Since then, Leroy's work ethic, or lack thereof, has done him no favors. His happy-go-lucky personality went through a swift metamorphosis into that of a sulky servant. It was the opposite of an ugly caterpillar transforming itself into an enchanting butterfly. Perhaps Mother was right; she usually is. After all, there is no other explanation. At the very least, I have to agree with Penny. He's an entirely different boy these days.

I sneak another glance out the window, and my heart sinks. Mother and Leroy are still out there. She's wagging her finger at him, and his chin hangs down to his chest. Then she points to the tobacco fields. He stumbles off in that direction, wiping his eyes on his sleeve and dragging his feet with every step.

With an ache in the pit of my stomach, I pull the coarse linen sheets off my bed. I remember the sense of satisfaction I felt weaving them myself. Now my glaring errors leap out at me, and I cringe. How I want to escape this drudgery. I picture myself out on the battlefield; it's my favorite daydream. There I am, risking my life to bring water to the quivering lips of wounded soldiers. Bullets whiz by me, yet I'm not deterred. Spotting an unmanned cannon, I race over to it and fire at the menacing Redcoats. When a smoking musket ball flies between my legs, I'm unfazed. Huzzah! It removes only the bottom row of my petticoat! Ah, I'm like Molly Pitcher when her husband collapsed during battle – at least in my daydream.

Within a split second, though, prickles of insecurity

invade my soul. Doubts flood my mind. I have such gall. What makes me believe I have that much courage? It's pure poppycock. Nothing has ever tested my inner mettle, not once. I shudder. Chances are I'd run willy-nilly to safety, deserting our cause for liberty without a backward glance.

Thankfully, Penny's throaty voice whisks me back to reality. "Miss Sukey, you hear that? Somebody be coming down the lane. Who the mistress expecting today?"

"We aren't expecting anyone. Well, at least I don't think so." I pause and shrug. "After all, nothing ever happens here. We should call it Nowhere Point." But the mere possibility of some excitement perks me up. I cock my head and pause. "I can't imagine who it could be."

The thundering hooves grow louder. My heart pounds along in a matching cadence. "Dear God," I breathe. "I pray this isn't a messenger delivering bad news." Covering my face with my hands, I sink onto my straw mattress and moan. "I'm too afraid to even look." Then peeking between my fingers, I whisper, "Please come with me."

My insides lurch as we run to the window. Confirming my worst fear, the gentleman on the horse looks like he's from the trading post. After all, there would be no other reason for a midday jaunt to Bollingbrook. Nowadays, even a peddler with a wagon of wares is an unusual event. This gruesome war consumed all the able-bodied boys and men ages ago. It has also divided many families and made enemies of best friends and neighbors. As Mother says, we're living through the worst kind of civil war. There are no boundary lines beyond our fence.

Taking a deep breath, I grab my petticoat and clatter downstairs as if King George is chasing me. With Penny on my heels, I arrive on the front portico as an older man in brown trousers and a matching vest comes around the bend into full view. It's the most terrifying messenger of all, Mister

Jones. After all, he owns the Peter Jones Trading Station. More importantly, though, he's the news coordinator for the Continental Army and Virginia militia depots in Petersburg. He was a dear friend of Father's, so surely any news he'd take the time to deliver himself must be dire.

I stand there gawking, bracing myself for the worst. My body tingles all over, yet I feel numb inside. Perhaps Stith is dead, or maybe it's Alexander. Even worse, maybe they're both gone. We'll soon find out whether we want to or not. But where is Mother? Why isn't she out here, too?

With a tight-lipped smile, Mister Jones dismounts from his horse. Then he nods to me as he tips his tricorne hat. It's all I can do not to tumble down the steps.

"Well, hello there, Miss Susanna. You look like you've seen an evil spirit." He pats my shoulder. "No worries, my dear. I've come with a letter and my glad tidings, of course. It appears to be from Stith. We just received our first delivery from North Carolina since the Battle of Guilford Court-house, so I wanted to get it to you right away. Strangely enough, there was a lull back at the station, so I decided to enjoy this fine spring weather and deliver it myself. I'm not often free to ride out here to God's country." He sighs, gazing over the bluff at the sparkling Appomattox River below. "If there's a lovelier spot in Virginia, I have yet to see it."

Mister Jones makes a slight bow toward our family ceme-tery. Although I was only four at the time of Father's burial, I still remember my heart swelling for Mister Jones. Neither Mother nor my brothers could bring themselves to shovel the dirt onto Father's grave, so he stepped forward and filled the void without a word. Afterward, he turned away, but I craned my neck to observe him. There he was, mopping his red-rimmed eyes with his handkerchief, ignoring the sweat pouring down his face.

He pulls a battered envelope from his waistband and

hands it to me with an affectionate squeeze to my wrist. I immediately drop my head and scan it. It's addressed to Mistress Susanna Bolling. Now I'm desperate to verify the return address. Sure enough, it reads, "Captain Stith Bolling, Commander, Company B, First Continental Light Dragoons."

It's from Stith!

CHAPTER 2
THE PRECIOUS LETTER

I'm woozy with elation. My twitching hands hold something magical: fresh news from Stith! Relief floods through my body like the warmth of a compress on an aching muscle. Surely he'll tell us that Alexander has survived as well! As much as I hate to admit it, my brothers' familiar faces have grown hazy. Over the years, their leave between enlistments has been rare, and often during the harvest when we are in need of every hand.

For the last couple of years, Stith has refused to take leave altogether. In a letter, he revealed the truth — that if he allowed himself to come home, he didn't trust himself to go back. I was crestfallen but admired his honesty. Looking back, I remember Mother clearing her throat several times after reading his revelation aloud. Despite the sadness clouding her eyes, she had paused for a moment and then declared, "He's a wise man to recognize his weakness and rise above it."

Bringing me back to the present moment, Mister Jones purses his lips. "Of course, I must remind you that the new casualty list is due in the morning. Hopefully this letter will dispel your worries, though." He beams as if he can't hold it in. "It's not often I get to share encouraging news these days, especially after such a deadly battle."

He extracts a news-sheet from his breast pocket. "And here's the latest *Virginia Gazette*. It's a few days old, but any information's a help these days." He winks. "Mistress Bolling might like to read General Greene's official report on Guilford Courthouse. It's reprinted from the *Independent Chronicle* up in Boston." He pulls out his pocket watch and gives it a glance. "I hate to appear rude, but I must return to the station before the post arrives. Please give your mother my best."

I'm giddy beyond belief, but I recall my manners and thank him. As he sets off with another tip of his hat, I glance down at the headline and grimace. "Massive Casualties from Guilford Courthouse Continue." A surge of panic runs through me. I refuse to give into it, certainly not with an unopened letter from Stith in hand. There's no better reason for confidence! If it says what I hope, then tomorrow's list won't apply to us. Nor will any others, not from this battle, anyway. I won't need to go to the trading station tomorrow after all. Huzzah for Mister Jones, and for the fresh hope he has delivered to our doorstep!

I stop and scold myself. There's still no guarantee this letter will contain good news. After all, we're at war and have been for years on end. Stith could've scrawled it from his deathbed.

Nevertheless, I'm far too excited to act like a lady. Finally, we have word from Stith and news of the battle as well. Waving the battered envelope, I dash into the house and holler like a stuck pig. "Mother! Mother, where are you?" I can't wait a minute longer to read this letter. But where, pray tell, is she?

Mother's house slave, Harriet, calls out, her squeaky voice muffled. "Miss Susanna, we way down here."

Suddenly it all makes sense. They're down in the tunnel. Of course, they couldn't hear Mister Jones arrive way out there. After all, it's a brick-lined passageway running from the cellar all the way out to the dock. With the help of our slaves, Father built it beneath the house to help protect us from Indian attacks. Nowadays we use it to bring goods up from the river. It's wide enough for the slaves to push wheelbarrows through, with lots of storage on either side. Regardless of the season, it's always the coolest place in the house. Stith and I spent many a scorching summer afternoon down in that earthy darkness, frightening each other with ghost stories. I was always the first to get spooked and hightail it out of there. He'd erupt into merry cackles as I'd run off wailing to Mother. What I wouldn't give for him to mock me again.

Mother calls out, her voice brimming with enthusiasm. "We've got the doors open at both ends. Even the tunnel can use fresh air on such a lovely day as this!"

I'm so preoccupied with the letter that her zest for cleaning doesn't make me cringe for once. I tear down the narrow steps, my heart floating like a dandelion seed in the wind. "Mother! Mother! We've got news!" The hazy lamplight outlines Harriet's stocky figure as I race toward the tunnel. "Mister Jones brought us a letter! It's from Stith! I can still tell his script anywhere!" I let out a giggle. What a moment to savor! I brush the letter back and forth across my thigh, burning to read its contents. "Well, they're more like scribbles, but they're his. That's all that matters."

"And that makes them the most beautiful of all!" Mother beams, as she emerges from the tunnel with her lantern held high. "What wonderful news! Come here, Sukey. Let's see what he has to say for himself!"

I rush over to her, my hands shaking as I pry open the

sealing wax. Then I fumble to unfold the torn, coarse paper. Suddenly I'm struck by the sharp odor of vinegar, and I wrinkle my nose. Finally, I hold the letter up to the flickering lantern with shaking hands. Unfortunately, Stith's words are so smudged that I can hardly make them out. But even that can't stifle the unbridled joy that courses through my body. If nothing else, Stith and I both touched the same piece of paper within the past month! I squint and stumble along, reading each word aloud as fast as I can decipher it. I'm barely able to keep myself from skipping straight to the end.

14 MARCH 1781

Dear Mother and Sister,

My apologies for the long passage of time. We've been short of paper, quills, time, and even a means to post letters, for an eternity it seems. At this moment I am immensely grateful for the chance to write and the ability to do so. Most have neither. Chances are this letter may never find its way into your hands. Unfortunately that's all quite commonplace these days. At the very least, I've savored this quiet moment to retrieve my scattered thoughts and think of you both with utmost fondness.

I detest starting off with a litany of complaints, though we are in a truly pitiful condition and about as disheartened as any men could be. When fortune is with us, we dine upon gators, frogs, or any critter unlucky enough to encounter us. However, our hardscrabble Continental Army is now not only hungry and forlorn, but almost naked as well. Indeed, the bulk of my men are shirtless, barefoot, and destitute of all other clothing, especially blankets. When an ailing soldier dies, he's carried off to a mass grave. Then another poor injured soul moves right into his dirty bed.

Without fail, General Greene has us on the move daily. He is indeed a Fighting Quaker! Every day we provoke skirmishes with General Cornwallis from behind cover, and then dive back into the woods before things can escalate. It's been a cat-and-mouse game for ages, and quite a successful one at that, slowing Cornwallis's stampede up through the South down to a crawl.

By now, I suppose you both know General Greene's motto well. "We fight, get beat, rise, and fight again!" Indeed it's true and really our only option other than outright surrender. Aye, he's worn down our enemy, but egad, we've exhausted ourselves in the process as well. We can't give up, though, as appealing as that may be; I couldn't bear to face either of you if we did. I bolster my spirits with General Washington's words. "We can win this war if we don't outright lose it." And so it continues, as it must. We have, all of us, sacrificed too much to buckle under now.

However, tomorrow the general shall lead us in our first big stand. We will face the fearsome Cornwallis and his entire British Southern Army in a tiny town out in the backcountry called Guilford Courthouse. It's far smaller than even our beloved City Point. I know you think it impossible, Sukey girl, but it's true! No doubt this will result in many a casualty, so I'll send this off this evening should something dire happen. After all, everyone knows any officer worth his salt leads from the front. I can't ask my soldiers to undertake anything I'm not brave enough to do myself. In my heart, I know Father would agree. I must remain upbeat. I've survived thus far with just a few fevers and a single bayonet wound to the thigh, and see absolutely no reason for my luck to change.

As you can imagine, I am conscience-stricken for neglecting to mention my wound last year. Honestly it was no cause for your concern. The area healed well without any infection or need for amputation, unlike so many other sorry chaps. Their horrible screams echoing from the hospital tent will haunt my dreams forever.

I can only imagine how much you both fretted over Alexander's musket ball to the shoulder. He'll always have my respect for demanding the surgeon set it aside for use in his next battle. Now I encourage my own soldiers to do the same.

Rest assured, Joseph and I shall do you right as the proud Conti-

nental Cavaliers that we are. Having my oldest friend in the world here with me provides a comfort I cannot describe. With him, I always have a bit of home by my side. Am I allowed to call him my best friend, or would that still make you cross, Sukey girl? Please know, sister, I could not miss you more.

Last I knew, Alexander was somewhere in the area. It's so dense with troops here and their constant movement that any chance of finding him is like grabbing a fish in your hands while swatting a mosquito. Oh, if only we were fishing in the Appo River right now or riding for sport without fear of an ambush. Wish 'twas within my power to provide you with more details, which you surely must crave.

By word of rumor, we've heard that Peter Francisco may join us this evening, ripe for battle as always. Bully for him, and bully for us with our Virginia Giant among us again. We could use him on our side now, more than ever.

My heart aches to return to Bollingbrook. How I'd love to see my favorite dogwoods blooming and roam our green fields. I'd even be thrilled to spend all day removing grubs from the tobacco plants! God willing, I shall write again soon. At long last Joseph summoned the nerve to write you as well, Sukey, but we simply haven't enough paper. I rib him that he must rid himself of the strange boils covering his body before he sees you again. In turn, he freely reminds me of my persistent body itch, a charge which I cannot deny. In fact, I can't tell you how many times I've scratched just while penning this letter. Perhaps I cannot count so high. Ah, what a pathetic pair we are! However, he does ask that I send his best to you both. We live by the words of Benjamin Franklin, "Fear not Death; for the sooner we die, the longer shall we be immortal." If only we could all linger here on earth a bit longer to anticipate our immortality, though!

If this letter smells a bit acidic, and you find my words blurred, know I've saved my last ration of vinegar to douse this paper before sending. I'd do anything to prevent spreading the bloody pox to you, Sukey. It's quite rampant here. In fact, General Washington himself declared it a greater threat than the sword. We've already suffered far

*too much from that dreadful disease with losing our dear Sallie, God
rest her soul.*

Your loving son and brother,
Stith

MY HEART PLUMMETS AS I LOWER THE PAPER IN A DAZE.
Mother and I stare at each another, our mouths hanging
open. Slowly, the shock sinks in, and she gives a heavy sigh.
It's so wonderful to hear from Stith after such an agonizing
silence, but in reality, his letter means nothing, not anymore.
We don't know if he survived the battle, or Alexander either.
Once again, I'm struck by how the tone of his letters has
changed over time. His upbeat ramblings on freedom from
tyranny have vanished, just like all our able-bodied men.

Even now, years later, any mention of Sallie still makes me
queasy. At the end, my precious little sister could no longer
see. That cruel disease blinded her before snuffing out her
young life. Since the pox is so dreadfully contagious, I never
got to say goodbye to her. Even after she passed, I longed to
curl her little hand in mine one last time, but poor Mother
couldn't allow me to do that. Even in death, Sallie's lifeless
body was still infectious.

Mother had insisted on nursing her, knowing full well
she'd contract the disease herself. Much to my relief, she
survived the ordeal. Pockmarks still scar her face and neck,
scattered about haphazardly with their unsightly pink craters.
I don't even notice them anymore, but Mother treasures each
and every one. They are her last connection to our dear Sallie.

With a grimace, I scan the news-sheet and pounce on an
article about Peter Francisco, the legendary Private hailing
from Buckingham County. His heroic actions in battle have
transformed him into a living legend. According to lore, he
once spotted a 1,100-pound cannon mired in mud after battle.

He singlehandedly hoisted it up onto his shoulder, and carried it off to keep it out of enemy hands.

VIRGINIA GIANT TRIUMPHS ONCE AGAIN – AT GUILFORD COURTHOUSE

Although between enlistments, Private Peter Francisco joined Colonel Watkins and his fellow Patriots down at the Battle of Guilford Courthouse. At 6 feet 8 inches, and 260 pounds, he is Virginia's largest soldier by far.

During the battle, this brave soul managed to kill eleven enemy grenadiers. According to several accounts, he earned himself yet another nickname, "The Virginia Hercules." He also brought great pain to many more of the enemy, including vengeance on the Regular who pierced his right thigh with a bayonet, entering above the knee and emerging from his hip socket. Following this injury, General Greene sent him home to recuperate. However, since Private Francisco had neither money nor a horse at his disposal, he limped along the entire 190-mile route.

At the age of five, Pvt. Francisco was found abandoned in City Point. Apparently abducted from a wealthy family in the Azores Islands, he spoke only Portuguese. Judge Anthony Winston of Buckingham County, an uncle of our former Governor Patrick Henry, later adopted him.

Despite his exemplary service, Francisco has refused to accept an officer's commission since he is unable to read or write.

I CLAP MY HANDS AND HOP UP AND DOWN. SO PETER Francisco did make it down there after all! He was quite a spectacle at last fall's spinning bee, this giant of a man hobbling on his injured leg from the Battle of Monmouth. Alas, he couldn't shuffle far anyway, since my cousin Betsy and a gaggle of her giggling girlfriends surrounded him the whole time. They hung on his every word as if he was General Washington. As much as I hate to admit it, though, I shouldn't criticize. I'd wanted to approach him as well, but was far too tongue-tied. With his swarthy olive skin, he was quite dashing, and surely the largest man I've ever encountered.

After that momentary distraction, the reality of the situation sets in. One thing is certain now. Tomorrow morning, Penny and I will, yet again, take a ride to the trading station at Market and West Old Streets. Once there, I'll wait on tenterhooks to see the new casualty list. Mother and I share this bone-chilling duty, alternating so one of us is home to mind Bollingbrook. Both roles are torturous in their own way. My breathing has already become shallower as I pray my brothers' names won't appear. Dear Lord, please help us avoid the Grim Reaper one more time.

My main concern is Stith. I don't dare voice that aloud, though, not even to Penny. I suffer pangs of guilt, but Alexander is a few years older. Plus Stith is Stith. Only two years apart, we grew up doing everything Mother would allow me as a girl, and often the forbidden too. Of course, that was until he and Alexander went off to war. Since then, nothing has been the same, and I doubt it ever will be, especially if he never returns home.

CHAPTER 3
GOOD NEWS AND HORRIBLE NEWS

The next morning Mother meets me for a prayer in the stable. After a tender embrace, I climb into the carriage, ready to face the trading station.

Penny murmurs, "Mistress Bolling, I ain't seen Leroy today. He been gone from the cabin since I woke up."

Mother clears her throat and frowns. I stiffen up, dreading her response. "Penny, I know he's your brother, but I just cannot have him in my home anymore." The color drains from Penny's face. "You see, yesterday my silver bracelet went missing." She speaks slowly as if to calm herself. "I've had it since it was handed down to me when I was a girl. It belonged to my grandmother, Pocahontas, whom I never met. It's especially precious because her father, Chief Powhatan, gave it to her. Of course, Leroy claims he had nothing to do with it, just like my brooch." Mother scoffs and shakes her head. "But once again, he was the only other person in my bedroom. Alas, my mind is made up." She sighs, and her tone roughens. "From now on, he shall work out in the fields. I don't have any other choice."

Penny's mouth hangs open. After a lengthy pause, she mutters, "Yes, ma'am."

And with that, she and I set off in an uneasy silence for the duration of our ride.

When we enter the trading station, I cast a nervous glance over the restless crowd. Spotting the scroll hanging on the shingled wall, I take in a ragged breath. There it is – the newest casualty list. As usual, it appears innocuous. I don't dare underestimate its power to decide life or death. I'm fully aware it can shatter my world with a single glance.

Gripping Penny's elbow, I press myself into the crowd. Spotting my cousin Betsy, I move in next to her despite my mixed feelings. But no matter how far I crane my neck, I can't catch a glimpse. As usual, the men in front block the view with their high, broad shoulders. I should be accustomed to this after so many years, but I can't help letting out a huff of indignation. My heart pounds at full force, and a wave of determination washes over me. I can't wait a minute longer; I must see it now despite the hordes of people in front of me.

Perched on my toes, I grab Betsy's shoulder with one hand and Penny's with the other. I thrust myself upward, but unfortunately the higher vantage point offers no real improvement. It's just as well, since Betsy shakes me off with a toss of her flaxen tresses. I smirk. If nothing else, I've succeeded in irritating her.

She purses her lips and glares at me. "Settle yourself, cousin. You look like a ninny with your ridiculous contortions. Remember you're a Bolling, so you'd best behave like one, not a silly tomboy." She lowers her voice into a snakelike hiss. "Such impertinence is not becoming of a lady of our station. We shall find out soon enough."

I want to ignore her, but her chiding just agitates me all the more. Gritting my teeth, I clench my apron and whisper to Penny, "Why does Mother assume we're friends? We're cousins and cousins only! Why can't she get that through her head?" I've always been more comfortable with boys anyway. That's except for Penny and my two sisters who are up in heaven with Father.

Within seconds my frustration gets the better of me. I fume aloud in a rowdy voice, daring it to carry. "Confound it! This is all so unfair!" If Father were still alive, no doubt they'd clear the way for him! He was among the first in Virginia's General Assembly to speak out against King George, long before the Boston Tea Party. Even though he's been gone a whole decade now, my heart aches for him. I still miss his massive bear hugs and him hoisting me up in the air, marveling how I've grown taller than him. I often comfort myself by imagining him embracing me through the lofty walls of Bollingbrook that he built with such devotion.

I all but bellow, "Don't I have as much right as the men to find out if my brothers are dead? Aren't we all part of the same cause?" The disapproving looks from the crowd don't bother me a bit. Acting like a lady isn't getting me any closer, just as it prevents me from contributing to this God-awful war. If I were a boy, everything would be different. I could risk my life on the battlefield, too. I'd no longer be a spec-tator relegated to the back of the crowd. With its typical stealth, though, self-doubt creeps into the cobwebs of my mind. Do I really have the courage? If the Redcoats actually shot at me, would I return fire? Or would I drop my musket and run away squealing? I sigh. There's no way to know until it happens, but my misgivings make it seem all the more likely.

Penny nods her head. "Let's just give it a minute, and we'll get you up there. You'll see."

Betsy shakes her curly blonde ringlets with an exaggerated sniff. "You're not the only one wanting to see the list, cousin.

You'll just have to wait like the rest of us. Well, except for me." The corners of her mouth turn up into a simpering smile, and I want to box her ears. "You're too young to understand this, but I'm eighteen and on the verge of becoming an old maid. So I'm in no hurry to find out how many more boys won't return home to court me."

Although I try to block out her blather, I roll my eyes. Oblivious to my reaction, she flashes her signature coy smile. "After all, there's only one boy who really matters to me. I'm so relieved that he wasn't near Guilford Courthouse, or even in North Carolina at all."

Of course, I don't need to ask about the boy's identity. Her pining for Peter Francisco has been no secret since last fall's spinning bee. In fact, she rarely talks about anything else, which I find revolting. With a smirk, I set out to deflate her.

"Oh yes, he was there. He most certainly was." I keep my tone light, confident my nonchalance will provoke her all the more. "And he was injured, quite badly in fact." I shake my head. "What a pity."

Betsy glowers at me with flaring nostrils. "And how would you know of all people? After all, you barely ever leave Bollingbrook." She curls her upper lip. "I happen to know he's home right now, between enlistments."

I toss my braid over my shoulder and shrug. Ignoring her snippiness, I do my best to irritate her further. "Stith told me – in a letter of course. Oh, it's also in this week's news-letter too."

"Really?" Betsy's baby blue eyes widen. "So you knew this, and you didn't bother to tell me?"

I shoot her a withering look. "Well, since you've barely met him, I didn't find the matter pressing." Of course I should've refrained from using such tart words, but a warm gloating feeling fills me as Betsy makes little puffing sounds.

At least a good row would spare me of her pestering for a bit. It's impossible to underestimate that value.

Up ahead, there's a chilling juxtaposition. The men who don't see familiar names on the list shout with glee while the unfortunate others break out in heaving sobs. The waiting crowd stands hushed and frozen with dread. It is a deathly quiet that speaks volumes, louder than dozens of cymbals smashed together. As many times as I've experienced this somber ritual, it never fails to shake me to the core. Alas, there's nothing to do but wait, but I have no such patience. Under my breath, I whisper, "Dear God, please spare him one more time – and Alexander too."

Mother's dear friend Mistress Blandford makes her way through the packed crowd and greets me with an affectionate smile. "Beautiful Susanna, I was hoping to see you here today! With those hazel eyes and ginger hair, you look more like your father every day. And what a handsome fellow he was. In this dim light, they look green as emeralds, your eyes do!"

She pats my arm, one of her many endearing traits. "Has your mother told you? Whenever my Joseph gets a letter through, he never fails to mention how well he's getting on with Stith." She chuckles. "Lately he's been asking about you, too, often before the rest of us."

I look away lest she see the scorn in my eyes. Mother reminds me of Joseph's newfound interest at every opportunity, but I can't muster any enthusiasm, not until my brothers have returned home unscathed. I know my heart should flutter at his interest, but I'm skeptical. After all, I've scarcely seen him in years. His freckled face, mischievous grin, and unruly red hair are blurry in my mind. Of course, he's been Stith's best friend since boyhood, but I'm still the little sister who pestered them.

"He's sixteen now, you see. I imagine he'll be looking to marry once he's back home." Her eyes sparkle. "The two of you would have such beautiful children! No doubt they'd be ginger-haired as well." Her cheeks turn a rosy pink as she beams.

Once Stith, Joseph, and I played a naughty prank on our tutor, hiding down in the tunnel for an entire lesson. Even though I was a tomboy, they only included me because I threatened to tattle. I blink, reliving the sting of Mother's whip afterwards. Nonetheless I still had no desire to sit with the ladies doing needlework or stitching a sampler. As much as I hate to admit it, it's no wonder Betsy developed into an excellent seamstress, while my stitches are still a haphazard mess.

Joseph spent so much time with us at Bollingbrook that Mother called him her third son. He paid me little mind as I tagged along, only mocking me when I snuck into Stith's trousers and had to yank them up after every step. He did teach me to paddle, though. How I basked in his attention! Thanks to him, I finally learned to keep my canoe on a straight path. But the world was a different place back then. The only thing that matters to me now is breaking through this crowd.

Given Betsy's constant whining about her impending old maid status, I should feel nothing but gratitude. Having a suitor these days is nothing short of a miracle with such a lack of eligible young men. After years of war, the widows and old maids outnumber the matrons by far. Once back home, Joseph could have his pick of many young ladies desperate for betrothal, and widows as well.

Mistress Blandford waves her hands. "This will all be over soon. I'm sure of it."

I avert my eyes and hold back a grimace. If only it was so simple! You can't just wish the war away like you're blowing out a lantern. Should it end soon, that would mean victory for the Redcoats. After all, they're on the verge of crushing us.

My mind races ahead, already tormented by King George's certain vengeance on the ruffians who dared to defy him, including Stith.

Perhaps Mistress Blandford is just mad. For the life of me, I can't fathom her unflappable confidence. How does she know that Joseph will return home in one piece?

After all, she lost her older son early on. Maybe she thinks Fate couldn't be so cruel as to take her remaining son. I want to shake her by her shoulders and scold her. *Madam, if you haven't noticed, unspeakable horrors take place every day and have been for years on end! Many a family has lost multiple members! Just look at Mistress Higgins who lost it all, her husband and both sons. She's bitter beyond recognition with a scowl all but tattooed on her face.*

Then again, maybe I'm the one who is daft. After all, I can't stop worrying about Stith and Alexander. I'm so plagued with nightmares that I'm afraid to drift off to sleep. So many questions gnaw at me, but I'm afraid of the answers. Where are they? How are they? Are they hungry? Do they have clothes? Do they have shoes? Are they injured? Are they dying? And then there's the worst question of all. Are they already dead? There's no way to guarantee they'll make it home alive and intact. My inability to help them, and our cause, rankles me to no end. I want to make my mark on the war. Alas, I cannot. Perhaps that saves me from discovering that I'm anything but brave.

Given the dismal circumstances, I'm resigned to worry as a constant part of daily life. Why isn't Mistress Blandford aware that our cause is so very desperate right now? General Cornwallis is ready to snuff it out once and for all! His mighty British Southern Army has swept north Savannah, leaving nothing but destruction in its path.

Ignoring the truth doesn't change it any. It just makes it more painful to accept later on. Doesn't the thought of hand-to-hand fighting at Guilford Courthouse take her breath away, too? Many of our soldiers fought buck-naked, with hardly a shred of clothing on their backs. Goodness me, some wore just their flint boxes, only big enough to cover their private parts. There weren't even enough muskets to go around. They had to wait for a fellow soldier to die. The thought of receiving a fallen Patriot's weapon, still warm and slippery with crimson ooze, makes me squirm.

An old man stands frozen up in front of the list. Suddenly his burly shoulders melt. Within seconds his entire upper body crumples inward. "Dear God," he wails as if he's alone in the cavernous room. "Not Henry! Dear God, no! Not this! He's only 17!"

As if by instinct, the men surrounding him back up a step. They are feigning politeness, but I wonder if they're also afraid his loss is as contagious as the pox. Finally a Good Samaritan helps the old man shuffle to the side as his body erupts in heaving sobs. Spotting some open space, I scoop up my petticoat and charge ahead, worming my slender frame through the pack.

Betsy calls after me in a shrill voice laced with anger. "Susanna Bolling! You simply cannot do that! You must wait like a young lady or I shall have no choice but to tell my Aunt Susanna!"

I hiss a retort over my shoulder. "Tattle all you want, cousin! I don't give a fig! Even Benjamin Franklin says God helps those who help themselves!" No one, especially her, will stop me from wedging myself into that gap before it disappears.

I twist and push my way toward the front. When I pass Mistress Higgins, she glowers at me with narrowed eyes and launches into a scolding. "Why, aren't you an awfully cheeky thing? And I don't suppose your mother is here to witness such a fine display of your uppity Bolling manners."

I ignore her. We may be on the same side of this war, but she's no kindred spirit. Mother makes a habit of defending her, claiming the poor woman hasn't always been so sour, but that the combination of her heartbreaking losses and then having to sell her slaves to pay for the funerals ruined her. Why is she even here? After all, she has no one left at stake. I can't help but assume the worst: witnessing the pain of others softens her own.

Finally the list hangs right in front of me. Huzzah! I reach out with my trembling index finger and touch it. My knees quiver, and a wave of nausea washes over me. I try to breathe in the musty air, but my chest is too constricted for more than a shallow inhale. Now faced with the truth, I'm too terrified to confront it. My thoughts run hither and thither like a spooked horse. Perhaps I shouldn't look at the list after all. Then my brothers can't be dead, not to me, not yet anyway. If I do actually read their names up there, they'll be gone from that moment on, gone forevermore.

Breaking into a sweat, I resist the urge to retreat. It's time. I must know the truth, no matter what. Plus, Mother is agonizing at home, waiting for my report. Although my real focus is on Stith, if Alexander died, part of me would also die, too. I've seen it happen. When we lost Father, a bit of Mother perished along with him. All at once, she lost her husband, dearest friend, and cousin. And the same went for Sallie, as well as my older sister, Mary, and her unborn baby.

I gloss over the lengthy list of A's and scan the B's from the top. The further down I look, the more my hands shake. I rush down through the names, bracing myself for the worst.

Bennigan, Caleb - Roanoke
Benton, Philip - Richmond
Blandford, Joseph - City Point
Bolton, Andrew - Alexandria
Brady, Samuel - Williamsburg

I read the B's several times over and stare, trying to take it all in, but I don't see anything. Do I trust my eyes? Finally I'm sure; there are no Bollings on the list. Yes, praise God, we're safe once again! My brothers are out of harm's way – for now anyway, and my extended Bolling kin as well. I let out a huge sigh of relief, as heartfelt as every other during this hateful war. Mother and I have survived; at least, until the next list arrives.

I want to shout, stamp my heels on the creaky wooden floor, and break into a jig. However, this is no time to gloat, not when my neighbors are receiving the most devastating news of their lives. With flushed cheeks, I turn on my heel to make my way out, delighted to relinquish my coveted spot. Despite my elation though, something doesn't feel quite right. But I can't pinpoint why. Then again, everything feels amiss these days.

After a moment of hesitation, I whirl back around and scan through the B's again. I have no explanation for my compulsion. After all, I'm already certain my brothers aren't on there. Halfway through, I gasp and clap a hand over my mouth. *"Blandford, Joseph."* There it is, clear as could be. My euphoria disappears in an instant. Instead my heart aches for the unsuspecting Mistress Blandford waiting patiently somewhere in the crowd behind me. This news will shatter her bizarre confidence with the force of a dozen cannon balls and tear her heart into bleeding pieces. For her, the worst has happened again. Her second son is gone forever, as is Stith's dearest friend and fellow cavalryman.

Keeping my moist eyes cast down, I work my way back through the crowd, my long braid swinging behind me like a pendulum. Despite my internal numbness, I feel someone's hand touch my shoulder. Caught off guard, I scan the people packed around me, leery of everyone. I brace myself for another rebuke from Mistress Higgins. I may be guilty, but I'm still not a speck remorseful.

But to my dismay, it's far worse than Mistress Higgins' scowl. I am face to face with Mistress Blandford again. Her kind eyes are now cloudy and full of tumult as they bore into my skull. "My dear girl, what of your brothers? Are they safe?" Her wrinkled mouth unfolds into an apologetic smile.

I'm frozen at first, but manage to nod as if all is well. But it's not, absolutely not. "Yes, ma'am. For now they are, praise God." I look past her, squirming in my worn boots. For the life of me, I can't bear to witness the raw fear running rampant in her eyes.

Mistress Blandford lets out a hoarse whisper. "Bless your heart, my dear." Her eyes now dart across my drawn face, searching for clues. "Did you see him? Did you see my boy on there?"

I can't bear to tell her that her son is dead. It's too much of a blow to deliver right now, right here. Pretending to reflect for a moment, I struggle for words. How I wish I could say, *No, ma'am, most definitely not. He isn't on there.* But no, that would be a blatant lie and cruel beyond measure. Joseph isn't coming home, not ever. Alas, her dear boy will never marry me or anyone else. She can no longer dream of becoming a doting grandmother, until her young daughter grows up. Oh, the sadness of it all is too overwhelming for me to handle right now.

Mistress Bland-ford's eyes beseech me, now wild with unadulterated terror. Panic has ripped off the mask covering her true emotions, revealing a portal into her frightened soul. "Susanna, please spare me the torture of going up there. It feels like the executioner's block, only worse. After all, it's my son's neck at stake instead of my own." She lets out a heavy sigh and hangs her head. "Every time I wonder if our luck has run out again. There's no warning when the Grim Reaper will pay us another visit." Placing a hand to her chest, she softens her face. "Please tell me. Please, for Joseph." She lingers on his name, savoring the sound.

Looking down at the brass buckles on my boots, I falter. "Excuse me, ma'am." I fumble with my apron strings, stalling as I wrestle with my conscience. "In my haste to look for my brothers' names, I neglected to look for Joseph." My neck grows hot; I'm sure it's splotchy red. "My sincerest apologies." I blush, well aware my words are far from genuine. I probably look like a sunburned tomato.

A look of crazed bewilderment sweeps across Mistress Blandford's face and then disappears as she regains her composure. "We all have many a burden on our shoulders these days, don't we? I shall find out soon enough." Tears bubble over, nonetheless, trickling down her ashen face. She swats them away with the back of her hand. "Please forgive my weeping. I pray we've thwarted the angel of death again, too." She reaches out and squeezes my hand, caressing it with her thumb. "We must stay united behind our cause if we're to have any hope at all."

A surge of shame washes over me. It wasn't right to lie to her; I know it full well. But I just couldn't bring myself to tell her the truth. Misty-eyed, I nod. Patting my shoulder, Mistress Blandford forces a tight-lipped smile. "Well, we're all looking forward to the spring spinning bee. It's so wonderful of your mother to organize these year after year. We surely need a happy occasion, don't we?"

Somehow I muster a wan smile in return. Her brave attempt at keeping herself in good spirits is hard to handle. Inwardly, I cringe for what she will soon endure. With a light sweat on my brow, I finally emerge from the crowd, relieved to have space around me. Scanning the slaves lining the back wall, I make a beeline for Penny's petite silhouette. Thankfully, I dodge past Betsy huddled with some other nitwitted girls, no doubt gossiping about Peter Francisco and my uncouth behavior. I smirk. Well, at least I've provided good fodder for discussion.

An expectant look crosses Penny's dark brown face. "What's the news, Miss Sukey?"

I flash her a closed-mouth smile. "They're all right, thank God." Then I lean into her and grab her arm. "But hurry! Let's go as fast as we can, so we don't have to see her!"

Penny shuffles forward with a puzzled look, but I'm already racing toward the door.

CHAPTER 4
A PRETEND PICNIC

I speed by the mammoth brick fireplace, my breath heavy. Finally, the door is just a few yards from my grasp. I can't wait to escape this stale air and the heartbreak unfolding here. As usual, the shelves are all but bare. With the British blockade going on for years, I can hardly remember otherwise. Everything's in especially short supply now. It's just as well. With our rampant inflation, a thick wad of Continental bills isn't worth much more than its paper. Even the French, our beloved allies, make us pay for our military supplies in the form of tobacco, and no one could blame them.

Just as I grab the door handle, an affable male voice rings out behind me. "Well, hello there, Miss Susanna!" Reluctantly I turn.

Mister Jones beams at me from behind the counter.

I wince before I can stop myself and hope he doesn't notice. As much as I long to escape out the door, I plaster on a smile and curtsy to him. I can't ignore his pleasantries, not after all he's done for my family. "Mister Jones, we thank you so much for the letter from Stith. What a wonderful surprise and so kind of you to deliver. We understand how busy you are."

"Happy to be of service. It's quite gratifying for me to deliver good news once in a while." Pausing, he cocks his head. "At least I hope it was good."

"Oh, yes, quite a relief." I flash him a smile. "But Stith wrote on the eve of the battle, so I came today to be sure."

"My wife and daughter are looking forward to your mother's spinning bee. I dare say they'll make it even if Benedict Arnold himself tries to stop them!" I know he jests, but my jaw tightens at the very mention of Arnold's name. The Great Turncoat's high treason of last September still rankles with me. I can't understand how he could so profoundly betray his fellow Americans. Oh, the nerve of it all; trying to sell West Point to the Brits!

I still smolder, knowing how angry Father would've been. Even worse, Arnold tried to arrange General Washington's capture in exchange for more quid! If his unthinkable plot had succeeded, the Redcoats would've executed our Commander-in-Chief. I shudder at the thought. How could Arnold do such a despicable thing? And now the louse is down here in Virginia slinking up and down the James River, wreaking havoc on his former compatriots. What an outrage! He's as depraved as Judas selling the Lord for some silver. Actually, he's even worse. At least Judas had the decency to hang himself.

Unfortunately, Arnold's raid on Richmond back in January was an embarrassing romp. Since the entire Virginia militia was down in North Carolina, Governor Jefferson couldn't do anything to resist the aggression. Nonetheless, he suffered ridicule for our weak showing.

"I declare they've saved up their words all winter long to visit with you ladies, while helping the cause," Mister Jones chuckles. "I'm willing to bet Lady Washington's famous spinning bees up at Mount Vernon aren't nearly as anticipated! I'm intrigued to learn the winners of this month's contest. I dare say it's your turn soon, Susanna!"

By now I'm tapping my foot, wanting to escape this jabber with all my being. When he leaves the counter and approaches me, it takes all my self-control not to scream in frustration. Cupping his hand to his mouth, he speaks in a hushed voice.

"Sometimes I get in little snippets from the depots, you see." He pauses to look over both his shoulders. "Should I hear anything about your brothers, I'll get word to you right away. We should start getting lists of the wounded soon. That's once they finish with the casualties, of course. Rest assured I'll take another ride to Bollingbrook should the need arise, whether I'm busy or not."

I force a polite smile. "Many thanks, Mister Jones. That's quite gracious of you." My initial euphoria recedes. Of course, any news worthy of another visit would be devastating. Nowadays, nothing is certain. Perhaps my brothers are part of the backlog and haven't made it onto the list yet. Even if they're still alive, they could be hovering on the brink of death. Perhaps they're suffering a grisly amputation right now, biting on musket balls to offset the pain. My jaw tightens again with a dull ache.

"I dare say it can't be easy for you and Mistress Bolling with the boys away for so long. Please give her my best."

"Mother will surely appreciate your thoughtfulness." Seeing my opportunity, I bid him farewell and grab Penny's elbow. "We must leave now before Mistress Blandford sees the list!"

Letting the door slam behind us, I set out at a fast trot toward the hitching post.

Two paces behind me, Penny murmurs, "Miss Sukey, if the boys are all right, why we hurrying away from her?" She gasps, and her face freezes. "You seen Mister Joseph up there! Ain't that right?"

All I can do is nod. Then words burst out of my mouth like bullets. "It's cruel and selfish, I know. But I couldn't tell her. I just couldn't. Not after she said Joseph wanted to marry me. I just couldn't stand the shock of it all. I couldn't bear to see her pain." I lower my head. "I'll pay my respects later, of course."

Penny stops moving mid-step. "Miss Sukey, what you saying?" After a deep gulp, she races to catch up to me. "Mister Joseph, he been killed?"

When I give a solemn nod, her eyes well up with tears. "Oh, it can't be true, not after him safe all this time!" Tears pour down her face. "Lord have mercy. We been knowing him since we was young 'uns playing on the river. Your mama going to be so sad."

Now I swallow over and over again, trying to hold myself together. "I saw his name up there myself, clear as a barrel full of rain water." Nonetheless tears gather in my eyes, too, threatening to spill over in a waterfall. Alas, we've lost another brave boy, someone I once knew and idolized. Perhaps he would've been my husband and the father of my children, but now I'll never know. What a godforsaken waste! This ghastly war creates nothing but heartache for everyone it touches. And somehow its malicious tentacles manage to reach everyone.

As we pass by Mitchell's Tavern, a group of men are engaged in a heated discussion. Most stand with a cane or crutches. It's the unfortunate norm for the men here at home; they're either too old to fight, or maimed from battle. Intrigued, I cock my head and raise a brow to Penny as she dries her tears on her apron. Surely they're discussing the war. They have to be. After all, there's nothing else to talk about. It's dominated every aspect of our lives for years now. Perhaps they have news; I'm determined to find out. Like Governor Jefferson once said, "Knowledge is power."

I survey the sun shining overhead and announce, "I'm famished. How about a picnic right here? It's close to noon after all." Then I vow to head home right afterwards and face Mother with the dreadful news.

Penny points to a grassy area. "Yes, this sure does look like a mighty fine spot." She sets off, calling back over her shoulder with a pointed look. "Don't you worry about nothing, Miss Sukey. Please do take your rest! I'll fetch the basket."

I seat myself on the grass and pretend to wait for Penny with our nonexistent basket. A few disinterested glances wash over me, and I catch a few glares out of the corner of my eye. Soon enough, though, they dismiss me. For the first time in my life, the presumption that I'm a simple-minded girl delights me to no end. I am right where I want to be without an iota of suspicion; not yet, anyway.

Keeping my head down, I poke a stick in the dirt, setting up the grid to play noughts and crosses. Like just about everything these days, it stirs up bittersweet memories of Stith. He was always X, and I was O. Of course, I lost every game until I learned to take the corners first. These days I'd give anything for him to wallop me and boast about it for days.

An older gentleman's voice rings out. Right away I recognize Mister Billingham, a cantankerous crony of Father's.

"Well, I'll be. Now even more of our boys are gone forever. Hang this blasted Revolution! What a godforsaken waste of the flesh of our youth!" He wags his head. "Tsk, tsk. How much does this liberty nonsense matter if none of our boys survive the war to enjoy it?" I flinch but still can't stop hanging on his every word.

His rant continues, and his anger becomes explosive. "Will these casualty lists ever stop coming? What a God-awful slaughter pen down there at Guilford Courthouse! More soldiers died there than they have townspeople! It'll be a wonder if any boys come home in one piece at the end of this war. At this rate, pretty girls like this one here won't have anyone left to marry."

The group turns to gawk at me. My cheeks grow hot, but I refuse to look up. The irony doesn't escape me. If my dwindling marriage prospects worry even this crotchety old man, perhaps Betsy isn't so wrong to complain all the time.

A young man with one arm speaks up. "Cornwallis may have declared victory down there, but nothing's changed! Let's keep the faith. The fight's still on for North Carolina! It's all thanks to Patriots down there who keep cutting their supply lines. And that's good news for us. Until Cornwallis gets total control, he can't even think about moving up here to Virginia." He surveys the group with a glib smile. "I don't know about you folks, but that sure makes me sleep easier at night."

A deep voice interjects from the back. "Well, if any good came out of that battle, their losses were far worse. Cornwallis lost a quarter of his men in ninety minutes! You hear that? A whole quarter of his army! Is he daft? How can he call that a victory, especially when they outnumbered us two-to-one? That's what I call a rout."

A man in the center chimes in. "And another quarter got injured, too! Plus his second-in-command O'Hara, and even that blasted Bloody Ban lost a couple of fingers! Huzzah! And they've plumb run out of supplies and ammo!"

On the far side, a slovenly young man with unruly jet-black hair hops away from the group. Then he takes an exaggerated bow toward the tiny stump where his left leg used to extend. "Gentlemen, where there was once a leg, you will now find air." He doesn't look familiar to me at first, but then in a flash I recognize him. He's Michael Farmer, Alexander's old chum, once the handsomest boy in Prince George County. "Hope every last one of 'em gets to join my club. Welcome to being useless as a babe! A leg or an arm sure ain't going to grow back for nobody. That silly King of theirs can issue all the infernal proclamations he wants. It's about as likely as pouring yourself a nice cup of tea from the bottom of Boston Harbor."

He lets out a bitter laugh and spits with a loud thwat. "And here I am back at home with loads of young ladies all about, but no one will have me." He gestures to his lost limb again. "Not now, not like this. Can't blame them none. Can't plow. Can't do nothing to provide. Can't even ride a darn horse anymore." He spits again with even more vigor. I can't help cringing.

Using his cane, he hops several times to change positions. From the fleeting glimpses that I dare take, I can see his awkward jerking motions bear no likeness to his former masculine bearing. Much to my dismay, he now faces me. His piercing blue eyes narrow in.

"Isn't that right, Susanna?"

Speechless, I hesitate. Then I look up and meet his glare, while the other men stare.

"Don't think I don't know who you are. You're Alexander's baby sis, the one who was always begging for piggyback rides." With considerable effort, he hobbles over to me. Up close he looks a fright. His face is covered in blemishes, and his eyes are bloodshot. Even worse, his clothes are rumpled and filthy as if he's slept in them for days. To make matters worse, his nose shines a cherry red. "You don't want to marry me, do you, Susanna?"

My mouth hangs open. I'm horrified, and I can't muster a response.

"You see, gentlemen! I was right." He beats his crutch on the ground. "Darn it! I stared death in the face at Saratoga. I wish that Lobster had shot me dead then! We'd all be better off. There's no point in living half a life." An uncomfortable pall falls over the hushed group.

I'm appalled. I sit frozen, holding my breath and wanting to vanish.

Mr. Billingham storms over to me and shakes a fleshy finger in my face. "Come to think of it, missy, that maid of yours has been gone an awful long time. You'd best get a handle on that Negro and not let her wander around unattended any longer. It just don't look right! If she doesn't run off and join the enemy, you'll outright spoil her rotten. I reckon you've heard more talk than you can understand for one day anyway. Run along now, young lady, while we men concentrate on the important matters of politics!"

Although tempted to fire off a saucy retort, I hold my tongue. Above all else, I don't want my unladylike actions reported back to Mother. With my cheeks burning, I take my time standing up and dusting off my gown. Then I force myself to amble off at a leisurely pace with my chin held high. To save the smidgen of pride I have left, I pretend he hasn't just run me off.

And yes, Michael Farmer was indeed correct. No, I don't want to marry him, not anymore anyway. While I once admired everything about him, all that remains is a smattering of pity outweighed by a heaping dose of revulsion. For that recipe, a wave of shame washes over me. But for now, I must get home to Mother and give her the good news. And then I will break her heart.

CHAPTER 5

BACK TO BOLLINGBROOK

P enny stands waiting next to the carriage, and relief washes over me. Since there is no one else in the vicinity, I shout out my complaints as I approach. I can't hold it in a second longer. "Why is it that just because I'm a girl everyone assumes I'm feeble-minded as well?" Of course, I won't tell Penny about Mr. Billingham's nasty comments about her. Although offensive, they're hardly unusual. Mother's treatment of our slaves differs from most owners. She strives for a balance between utmost firmness and kindness. It's a rarity, but she believes all people are made in the likeness of God. If only everyone else believed that as well.

"I got you, Miss Sukey. Most white people don't think Negroes even got a brain in their heads."

I stop short, realizing Penny has it far worse than I could ever fathom. Disgusted with myself, I grab hold of the reins. I so dread telling Mother about Joseph; losing him will come as such a colossal blow to her. Nevertheless, I'm the messenger. There's no way to avoid it this time.

Despite my obligation to share the sorrowful news, I can't

help savoring the fact that my brothers are safe, for now. Huzzah! As we round the bend into Bollingbrook, I can finally take notice of our new green crops popping up all over the farmland, one of my favorite sights. I'm so happy the harsh winter is officially over. Our blooming Virginia dogwood trees perfume the air. Carpets of lush greenery border the dirt-brown fields with a myriad of wildflowers. Rose milkweed, blue chicory, and downy yellow foxglove explode in a kaleidoscope of color. Guilt plagues me for finding joy in anything with Joseph so freshly gone from this earth.

Once again, Big Hank has nurtured the tobacco seeds over the winter with his usual rousing success. Slaves wearing kerchiefs and broad-brimmed hats are scattered about in small gangs, stooped over, planting the leafy green seedlings on knee-high mounds of soil. From now on, they'll inspect each leaf every morning until harvest and remove the pesky grubs with tender care. Otherwise, those tiny beetles will nibble the plants away and eventually destroy our entire crop.

As our plantation's trusted slave driver, Big Hank prides himself on producing the most bountiful crop in the Tidewater area. He's a towering man with muscular shoulders and rough skin of deep mahogany. Despite his imposing presence, he's known for his good nature and fairness. Mother tells me I was terrified of him when I was young, but nowadays he's my rock.

This year, these fresh seedlings are especially precious. Every planter in the Tidewater area is on tenterhooks, still waiting to cash in on last year's harvest. Determined to starve us economically, the Brits intensified their blockade over the winter. As a result, all the hogsheads full of tobacco remain in our Bolling inspection warehouses, still unsold to the French.

Thankfully, in February, we received an answer to our fervent prayers. General Lafayette returned from France with more financial support and soldiers. In addition, he pledged that a fleet of French ships would arrive in Chesapeake Bay within months. On their return, they will escort our tobacco back to France! And there is yet another reason to rejoice. General Washington sent General Lafayette here to lead Virginia. Now he is our defender from the repulsive Benedict Arnold. Huzzah!

As we head toward the stable, though, dread overcomes me. I jump off the carriage before it comes to a full stop and toss the reins to Penny. Within seconds, Mother's angular form appears out of the shadows. Right away her ashen face is fixed on me. Harriet creeps out behind her with her eyes round as pumpkins. As our former nanny, she cried the hardest of all when the boys went off to war.

In a small yet authoritative voice, Mother asks, "What's the news, Sukey?" She smooths back her salt-and-pepper hair and jerks on her ruffled mobcap. "I haven't stopped praying since you left, and I've mucked every stall and even tidied up some." She presses her lips together in a straight line as she steels herself for the worst. The words catch in my throat; I'm unable to utter a sound. All I can do is stare at the tiny bits of straw sprinkled all over her gown.

"What is it, my dear? Why so forlorn?" She drops her chin and lowers her voice. "You must tell me now, Sukey, or I shall go mad! Surely it's not what I'm thinking!"

Harriet shrieks, "It ain't one of the boys, is it? Glory be to God, no!" She claps a hand over her mouth, but the raised scars crisscrossing her cheeks and neck are still prominent. Long before I was born, Father bought Harriet from a master notorious for daily floggings. Even now, she remains jittery on her best days.

Anxious to put Mother at ease, I force myself to spit out the good news. "Mother, they're all right, both of them." Now that I've started talking, I can't get the words out fast enough. They gush out in a torrent. "No, they weren't on the list – no Stith, no Alexander! I'm sure they weren't. And our Bolling name wasn't there at all." I let out a deep exhale. "We're the lucky ones. We've been spared again."

"Well, thanks be to God! We're all safe again, until next week," Mother cries, her eyes shining as she claps her hands together. As she embraces me, I bite my lip. I don't have the heart to tell her that Mister Jones can now find out casualties early. Then she'll tremble every time she hears a horse galloping toward Bollingbrook. Despite her dedication to the cause, she already has far more worries than any person should have to bear.

I force myself to continue. "But, Mother, here's something else. There's some very sad news, too."

Mother's bluish-gray eyes zoom in on me with piercing urgency. Instantly I become tongue-tied yet again. Finally, unable to think of a better way to say it, I blurt it out. "Joseph, he's gone! His name was on the list. Joseph Blandford. I'm sure it was there. I saw it myself." Although my eyes are downcast, I can feel Mother's open-mouthed gaze fixed upon me, and I squirm. I take in a long, ragged breath. "I was so worried about the boys that I forgot to look for him at first. But then I did. I couldn't believe it was real, but it was. *'Blandford, Joseph - City Point.'*"

My voice trails off, but I force myself to meet Mother's cloudy eyes. "I must confess something else to you, too. We left before Mistress Blandford found out." I look down at the dirt floor again. "I'm ashamed to admit it, but I just couldn't face her, not right then. I couldn't bear to see her grief so fresh." My throat closes up, choking me with self-recrimination.

Guilt washes over me. My partial confession is woefully inadequate. I left out the worst part, lying to dear Mistress Blandford who all but begged for my brutal honesty. This second falsehood to cover up my first is an additional wrong. By misleading Mother, I've lied again. But I just can't own up to my cowardly conduct, especially not to her. Finding out I deceived Mistress Blandford in her time of need would infuriate Mother beyond measure. I could've spared Mistress Blanford the agony of reading her precious son's name on a public casualty list. But no, consumed with selfishness, I refused. So much for my grandiose daydreams of bravery on the battlefield! I couldn't even treat a lovely woman with common decency at the trading post.

Mother is utterly gob-smacked. She gasps and raises her hands to her withered cheeks. "Dear God, no," she moans. "I remember the day he was born just as clear as Easter Sunday. He was just months after Stith. Oh, not our Joseph!" Her chest heaves under her worn gown. Tears spill over, but she doesn't notice. After several ragged breaths, she gives into her weeping, fanning herself with her calloused hands. Then she rubs Harriet's back as Harriet breaks into several long, shuddering sobs.

After a few moments, Mother regains her composure. "I shall go see Rebecca right away. I'll sit with her. Yes, that's what I must do."

She pauses.

"Oh dear, I must think of the right words to comfort the poor dear. She was such a blessing when we lost Mary and the baby." She shakes her head as if to escape the torturous memories of my older sister dying during childbirth. "Even the perfect words won't help today or many days hence." Mother mops her teary eyes with her yellowed apron. "I don't know why it's always such a shock when another boy dies. We are at war after all." She clenches her fists and lets out a moan. "Shouldn't we expect tragedy to befall us by now? I'm afraid our cause shall be the next to receive a fatal blow."

I'm unnerved. I've never seen her so rattled. She closes

her eyes for an extended moment and then snaps into action, doling out orders. "I shall take some goodies. Penny, have Auntie Ruth fill a basket of cornbread and anything else on hand. If you can't find her in the cookhouse, check the summer kitchen. She's moving some things out there today. Harriet, get the carriage ready. Then you and I will set out for the Blandfords'." Mother raises her index finger. "Now let's not dilly-dally! We must get there as soon as possible. There'll be time for you to inform everyone later."

As Harriet and Penny scuttle off, Mother brings a fist to her pursed lips. "Sukey, I shall leave you to ride out and find Big Hank. Check on how the planting is faring. Of course, I have no doubts. If anyone can get it done right, it's him with nary a word of complaint. I tell you, he's worth ten white men. It doesn't matter, though, since there aren't any for hire."

Mother wags her forefinger. "But before you head out, get Auntie Ruth started on the death cakes and plenty of them, too. Rebecca's servants will be overwhelmed with grief soon enough." Tradition requires the bereaved family to hand out special biscuit-cakes as a way to spread the sad news. "They won't have enough gloves or handkerchiefs to give everyone, so the funeral cakes will just have to do. Once the Blandfords make proper arrangements, we'll wrap them up in the death notice. Then we'll be Warners, knocking on doors and passing them out around town. It's such a dreadful task, but people do want to know. Well, at least the Patriots do anyway. Of course, the town crier will make his own public announcement. Mister Jones will spread the news as well. Being there at the trading station in the thick of it all makes him the best Warner in town." Mother fades into her own thoughts with a look of shock imprinted on her ashen face.

After a few minutes, she prattles on with practicalities. "Sukey, have Penny bring my black gown and bonnet over to the wash house, will you? And send yours as well." She gazes out over the fields. "It's a wonder we haven't worn them out by now, but we may yet." She speaks so softly I can barely make it out. "At this rate we may very well indeed." Her misty eyes droop, and her face darkens. "Oh, it's just despicable. I hope General Cornwallis has to answer to God for this one day soon. He doesn't even value his own soldiers' lives, and our boys even less. As the mother of two boys trying to stay alive on that battlefield, I find that awfully hard to accept." I shudder and hope Mother didn't notice.

CHAPTER 6

DEATH CAKES AND A THIRSTY MUSKET

With my mind whirling, I meander among our primitive outbuildings and follow the aroma of fresh bread into the intense heat of the kitchen. Within seconds, my eyes sting and itch from the hazy smoke trapped inside.

A shrunken Negro woman is stooping over a massive cast-iron pot, stirring a thick concoction with both hands. Raising her head, she greets me with a lopsided smile revealing a few crooked teeth. "Miss Sukey, I making your favorite parsnip an' turnip soup today."

Despite my somber mood, I can't help but grin. As long as I can remember, Auntie Ruth has been holding a wooden spoon, and today is no exception. As a youngster, I loved to bake with her, especially my favorite cornmeal spoon bread. I was convinced Auntie Ruth held a spoon even when she slept. After all, she'd need to stir the food she cooked in her dreams.

As the oldest person on Bollingbrook, Auntie Ruth has prepared meals in our massive fireplaces since before I was born. Despite coordinating everything with military precision, however, she has countless burns covering her gnarly hands. To this day, I've never seen Auntie Ruth's hair, only the tattered rags knotted on top of her head.

She mops her brow with her stained apron. "So, the mistress and Harriet done set off for the Blandfords?" Her wrinkled eyes hone in on my face, laced with concern. "Why, Miss Sukey, you look like you done seen a ghost!"

I hesitate, knowing how much this news will upset her. "Penny and I just came back from the trading station." I pause. "I don't know how to say this, Auntie Ruth. It's Mister Joseph. He's gone."

My voice trails off. There are no details, not yet, so unfortunately there's nothing more to say. I don't mean to be callous, but at this point they don't matter anyway. He's dead and gone forevermore. I close my eyes, marveling at the futility of war.

"Oh, that fine boy! What a shame." Auntie Ruth's eyes flood with tears. "Poor, poor Mistress Blandford." Her voice is soft but thick. "So now it be time for death cakes?"

"Yes." I speak just above a whisper.

Auntie Ruth shakes her head as tears trickle down the weathered grooves in her cheeks. "Usually I helping someone else with their death cakes. Glory be, not this time." She mops her cheeks. "Mister Joseph used to sneak in here begging for sweets all the time." She musters a sad smile, her eyes clouded with sorrow. "Now I be making him the best cakes anyone ever done tasted. I going to use all my molds and make them all kinds too - ginger, molasses, and caraway."

I can't utter a word lest I burst into tears myself. It's only halfway through the day, and I'm drained. Leaving Auntie Ruth to bake, I set off in search of Big Hank. As I mount my beloved horse Musket, my spirits can't help but rise. Nothing ever seems as bleak when I'm on horseback. Riding always reminds me of my many adventures with Stith. Once we'd escaped Mother's watchful eye, I always adjusted my saddle so I could straddle Musket like a boy. Then I'd change back to sidesaddle right before we returned.

I can't keep my mind from retreating into the past. *It was a steaming summer day, but we scarcely noticed. We galloped neck-to-neck around City Point, finishing in a dead heat, much to my delight. To break the tie, we raced canoes. Of course, Stith prevailed. As the winner he got to upend me, plunging me into the river. For the first few seconds, I reveled in the water's refreshing coolness. Quickly though, the weight of my gown and petticoat dragged me under. Within seconds, Stith's strong hands grabbed my shoulders and pulled me to the surface. Then he teased me for days.*

Alas, as much as I long for those days, they are long over. It's hard to believe that our lives were once so carefree, long before talk of war crossed anyone's lips. These days, my constant duties and the danger lurking everywhere don't allow for any frivolous riding. I can't recall my last long ride, even on Bollingbrook. Although I'll feel quite sore later on, the pleasure will be well worth it.

I smile as blustery winds inundate me with the delightful scents of springtime. Then with a start, I become conscious of my enjoyment and admonish myself. What a horrid creature I am to indulge myself at such a tragic time! The poor Blandford family is bearing the unbearable, no doubt struggling under the crushing weight of their grief. My thoughts return to Stith. I can only imagine his searing pain. All at once, he's lost a fellow officer and his closest friend since childhood.

It all seems so unfair. Yes, Joseph is dead, but the world goes on living as if he never existed, myself included. Releasing a heavy sigh, I pull in the reins, nudge Musket, and pick up the pace.

Gangs of slaves are spread out across the fields rooting the fledgling tobacco plants, but I don't see Big Hank anywhere. I ride across a few other fields growing wheat, flax and corn, but I don't catch a glimpse of him. Usually his hulking frame is impossible to miss, much like Peter Francisco, the Virginia Giant.

Overheated and parched beyond words, I stop at a supply shack. I dismount from Musket and stretch my legs. Standing over a bucket of water, I weave my fingers together and gulp down several handfuls, savoring every drop despite its warmth. Stepping aside, I leave the rest for poor Musket who's probably even thirstier than me. Sticking his nose deep into the bucket, he gulps it down as fast as he can. Leaning against the shack, I sink to the ground, my face hot. As I catch my breath, I savor the rich loamy scent of the freshly turned soil.

Nearby a Negro man shouts, startling me. "Don't you go telling me how much you done planted this morning! That's not what the rest of the gang done told me. You ain't done a lick, boy! There be no lying around here." The man is quite close, just on the other side of the shack. As the tirade continues, his angry voice sounds familiar. I can't believe it, but I could swear it's Big Hank. I've never heard him yell even while disciplining, so it's hard to know for sure. Come to think of it, he's never raised his voice around me. It just isn't his nature. He always wears the same easy smile showcasing the considerable gaps between his crooked teeth. The longer I listen, though, the more convinced I become. The angry man is definitely Big Hank, but I don't know who he is yelling at, or why.

"There ain't no reason to do all this work." Without a doubt it's a slave boy, but the voice is muffled. After some incoherent rambling, I make out some more words: "Them Bolling boys, they fight for their own freedom from the Brits, but not for us Negroes." He's sobbing now, his cries full of anguish. "We don't get no chance at freedom, never."

I'm taken aback. I had no idea any of our slaves harbored such resentment. I cringe, realizing I've never bothered to think about it.

Big Hank's voice booms, shaking with anger. "I don't like being nobody's slave neither, but I'm going to tell you something. If I got to be a slave and my children got to be slaves, I want to be their slave! Mistress Bolling, she been getting by all these years without her boys and working just as hard as us from sunlight to no light at all. All's she can do is treat us right, and that's what she do, and Miss Susanna, too."

The slave boy cries out. "We ain't got no privileges out here. We got nothing. I got a mind to set off on my own."

As I mop my brow with my apron, I cock my head. Did I hear him right? Is he threatening to run away? I can only imagine Mother's unbridled fury.

"Penny ain't a real slave, not like us." With a flash I know exactly who it is. It's Leroy! I should've guessed. "They got special rules up there in the big house, but now I'm a real slave working out in the sun every day."

I bite my lip; I can hardly disagree with him. This is a common complaint from the field slaves. They believe those Negroes who work inside the house receive better treatment. He should know better than anyone.

Big Hank is incensed. "I tell you what, Leroy! If we be free, where we be going then? All them Colonies got slaves, all of 'em. A slave catcher be grabbing our papers and selling us off, all alone, to some cruel masters down deep South. You understand me? We animals for sure then, and you won't ever see your sister again."

"But I ain't got freedom here! What about the Brits? They done promised to set us free if we help them. Them Patriots, they only want freedom for themselves."

"Well, I don't trust them lobsterback promises neither. What if they change their mind when the war be done and just send everyone back? They sure ain't going to bring them all to England on them fancy ships, that for sure. Boy, I don't ever want to hear any more such talk, or you getting a thrashing you won't ever forget! You hear me?"

Silence falls, followed by some sniffling.

Big Hank yells even louder. "Leroy! You hear me, boy?"

Leroy mumbles in a gravelly voice, "Uh-huh." He doesn't sound convinced, though.

"And I tell you something else, even worse! You know Mistress Bolling don't like to split no families. But if you giving her a hard time too long, you going to find yourself downriver mighty fast."

I'm so engrossed that I fail to notice Musket has run out of water. He knocks the bucket hard against the shed in hopes of loosening a few more drops. A loud crack rings out. I scramble to my feet, hoping to get away before they discover me.

Within seconds, though, Big Hank's dark face peeks around the corner. His eyes are as round as the full sun beating down on us. "Miss Susanna, we didn't know you was there!" His jaw hangs slack as he gapes at me without blinking.

I fake a wide, toothy smile. Then I struggle for something to say, anything. "Big Hank, I haven't been here but a moment really." Now I can't stop myself from babbling. "That silly Musket kicked the bucket over first thing. Mother had something pressing to handle, so she sent me out here to check on the planting." I hope I'm making at least an iota of sense. "Certainly looks like the beginnings of another healthy crop!"

Leroy slinks around the corner with his eyes cast downward. "Miss Susanna, I didn't mean nothing back there. Big Hank was trying to explain some things to me. Please, I don't want no trouble for me, or my sister either."

LIBBY CARTY MCNAMEE

"Not at all, Leroy. Musket and I must be heading back to the house. I'll be sure to tell Mother the planting is faring quite well as always." I can attest to that in all honesty.

Grabbing the reins, I remount Musket and retrace my route. In fact, that's all I'm going to say, especially to Penny. There's no need to upset her. I also don't want to inflict more shame on Leroy or interfere with Big Hank's discipline. Like everything else, he's got the situation well under control. Deep down, though, I can't blame Leroy for resenting his bondage. After all, what gives any person the right to own another? With a grimace, I shake my head.

There isn't anything to do about slavery, not right now anyway, even though General Washington and Governor Jefferson have both spoken out against it. Virginia law forbids Mother from freeing her slaves unless the General Assembly approves it, so Leroy will remain her property. The reality offers no relief either. Even if Mother had such authority, our fields would lie fallow. Eventually we'd face starvation as well as bankruptcy.

Unfortunately, Leroy is correct. His only hope to obtain his freedom is to run off and join the British. However, there's no way to know if they'll actually keep their promise until the war finally ends. Thankfully, the journey to find the enemy down in Portsmouth would be treacherous, making it nigh on impossible for one boy on his own. I find solace in that for everyone's sake. Of course, I'm choosing to ignore the looming threat of another of Arnold's raids.

CHAPTER 7
A SAD DAY

Clad in our mourning gowns, Mother and I ride down our meandering lane to Joseph's funeral at Blandfield. I glance at the menacing pewter-colored skies looming overhead; these gloomy clouds suit the melancholy occasion. Staring into my lap at my folded hands, I brace myself, resigned to shedding many tears. They're as inevitable as the impending storm. After one look at the devastated Mistress Blandford, I fear I'll release a fierce downpour of my own.

Mother's eyes remain puffy and red-rimmed, as they've been since she received the devastating news. Clad in a threadbare black chemise faded to a drab gray, Penny drives the carriage as huge tears roll down Auntie Ruth's shriveled face next to me. The rest of our slaves shuffle along behind us in somber silence, carrying baskets heaped with death cakes. Only one sound prevails over the clippety-clop of the horses' hooves: Harriet's wailing.

Holding my breath as we pass by several Tory farms with Union Jack flags snapping in the breeze, I sense people are gathered along the roadside, but I keep my gaze fixed down on my trembling hands. This is no time for trouble with those nasty Tories, not on the way to Joseph's funeral.

Lo and behold, jeers and booing ring out as we pass the Fredericks' farm. It quickly builds into a cacophony, making my heart pound. It's no secret they have supported the Crown since the hostilities started, just as fiercely as we've opposed it. Their oldest son, Thomas, was once best of chums with Stith and Joseph. However, their merry triumvirate ended abruptly when the war broke out. The boyhood friendship was severed like an axe splitting a log with one sharp crack.

In an instant our families became bitter enemies, unfortunately an all too common occurrence during these contentious times. Even Benjamin Franklin permanently cut ties with his Tory son, William, who was the Royal Governor of New Jersey. Thomas Frederick is now a Captain, the same rank as Stith. However, he fights on behalf of the King. It's still hard for me to accept that their idyllic friendship is over. Unlike most of my brothers' friends, Thomas was always cordial, entertaining my silly questions, and including me in their escapades.

Mister Frederick calls out in a low, menacing tone. "Hello there, traitorous Bollings! So you're on your way to yet another rebel funeral, are you?"

Without flinching, Mother stares ahead. Then she hisses at me through pursed lips. "Do not react! That's exactly what they want." She keeps her back ramrod straight as if she's bracing her body for further taunts. Her restraint amazes me. It must require every ounce of her energy to ignore him.

The shrill voice of Mistress Frederick rings out next, full of anguish. "Now young Joseph is gone, too! How many must die before you see reason, Mistress Bolling? Soon we'll have none of our boys left! And remember, you have two to lose. They could be next!"

I feel like I'm about to vomit. No one could say crueler words to me, but I stifle my horror.

Their daughter lets out a blood-curling shriek. "Another British win at Guilford Courthouse! Huzzah! Soon my brother shall return home in victory!"

Mister Frederick booms again. "You are a disgrace to His Majesty! You sorry traitors should be dragged off to London and hung!" I have never wanted to get out of somewhere so badly in my life.

It only gets worse. Mistress Frederick's voice takes on a savage fury. "Be rid of you, enemies of the Crown! May God have mercy on your treasonous souls."

There's a disgusting guttural sound; someone is gathering phlegm in his mouth. A thick wad lands next to my foot with a loud thwat, and my heart races. Thanks to Mother's warning, though, I don't move. I refuse to give them the satisfaction of seeing me recoil.

Mister Frederick takes over. "To all you sorry slaves, come to your senses before it's too late! Run for your lives! Join the British and gain your freedom! Otherwise you'll remain slaves forevermore!"

I have a powerful urge to turn and gage Leroy's reaction, but I repress it. I don't dare risk Mother's wrath. Nothing is worth that scourge.

Thankfully we soon pass our vile Tory hecklers. Within the cloud of dust swirling behind us, the girl screams, "Long live King George!" The words echo in my head as our entourage travels along in a dazed silence, even Harriet.

Our arrival at Blandfield comes as a welcome relief despite the tragic occasion. Townspeople clad in black fill the spacious lawn and surrounding fields. I nudge Penny and gesture to the expansive crowd.

"Look at all these people! What fine Warners we were! Why, even the town crier himself is here to pay his respects!"

Wearing black crepe armbands, slaves bustle out of the kitchen house, struggling under bountiful trays of fine food. Within minutes, steaming platters of roasted ham, chicken, and beef fill the long tables.

Mother surveys the throng of people. "What a fine tribute to Joseph even if we couldn't be at their family church." She nods her head in approval. "Aye, it appears every Patriot in the Tidewater area has come."

More slaves emerge from the cellar, rolling hogsheads of ale and cider in anticipation of a thirsty crowd. The slave children scurry about ferrying cornucopia baskets filled with sweet rolls and cakes. Regardless of the financial state of the bereaved, mourning is an expensive event. Tradition demands a generous spread, even if it is well beyond the family's means, as it is for almost everyone these days. Perhaps without such distraction, the sadness would be too overwhelming to handle.

I release a defeated sigh. "Why does it feel like we were just at a funeral yesterday?" Maybe Mister Frederick was right. Perhaps these senseless deaths will never end, and the relentless Grim Reaper will wield his murderous scythe until no men are left, including Stith and Alexander. I shudder. The Fredericks and I actually agree on at least one thing. We both despair over the waste of so many young lives.

With slumped shoulders, Penny frowns. "The last one was a fortnight ago, Benjamin Waters. It feel like yesterday because we seen so many." Her eyes mist over. "Goodness gracious, I lost count a long time ago."

The minister clears his throat and starts the ceremony in a commanding yet somber voice. I drift off into my own thoughts, shedding tears for Stith's best friend, and yet another fine Patriot lost. Of course, marrying Joseph could've been an ideal arrangement. Despite the fact he'd become a stranger of late, we shared too many ties to count. And

Mistress Blandford was right. Chances are we would've had beautiful red-headed babies. I smile ruefully despite my watery eyes. It might have been worth marrying Joseph just for Stith to be the third wheel for once. Thankfully I stifle my cackle before anyone thinks I've gone mad. None of it was ever meant to be, so there's no point in dwelling on it.

From a makeshift pulpit, the minister thunders out his eulogy as if the words have descended directly from the heavens. "Thomas Paine spoke the truth! These are indeed the times that try men's souls! Haven't we all seen too many 'summer soldiers' and 'sunshine Patriots' shrink from real service to our country? It's the true Patriots who sacrifice everything and deserve our utmost love and gratitude. Our beloved Joseph earned that as well as his family. Now they face an arduous task. They must summon the courage from deep within to continue their lives without him."

Mistress Blandford lets out a heartbreaking howl that makes me want to howl, too. Rocking back and forth in her seat, she keens for her second son. He's been lost for a cause that is all but lost as well. I can't help but hate myself for my weakness. She's entitled to her pain.

This preaching convicts me. I haven't lived up to my duty as a Patriot. I shrank from telling Mistress Blandford the truth, causing a fellow Daughter of Liberty to suffer more anguish. Surely real heroines like Molly Pitcher and Sybil Luddington would've faced such a task without focusing on their own discomfort. Alas, I most certainly did not.

I have no right to dream of fame and glory after my shameful behavior. In spite of my lofty daydreams, I proved myself yet another summer soldier and sunshine Patriot. Yes, the war certainly has tried my soul, but my burdens are far lighter than so many others. I hang my head. Weeping over a boy I barely know anymore doesn't count as a heart-wrenching loss.

When the service concludes, the crowd remains hushed. Mister Blandford trudges toward the ceremonial cannon up front, stooped over as if he carries its weight on his back. Plucking his handkerchief from his pocket, he wipes his face and fires it off with a jarring boom. He stares into the stormy sky as plumes of smoke waft through the air, breaking apart until they disappear. In a matter of moments, they're gone, just like Joseph. After drying his eyes a second time, Mister Blandford haltingly lumbers off, still weighed by his invisible burden.

Mother rushes to comfort the weeping Mistress Bland-ford with Mistresses Harrison and Bland. The other guests fan out onto the grass and survey the mouth-watering spread. Joseph's little sister Louise passes out Auntie Ruth's death cakes wrapped in the funeral notice, and offers a sip of spirits.

Betsy clings to my arm, sobbing into her lacey linen hand-kerchief. "Woe to us, cousin! Yet another potential beau is gone, and from such a fine family. Perhaps it's time for us to accept our destiny. Where have the girls gone with the cakes? Old maids don't have to keep a proper figure, so I may as well indulge myself."

My hand tingles with the intoxicating desire to box my dear cousin's ears. Instead I ask, "When did you last see Joseph?" I fight to keep my tone even, but there's an edge of bitterness, nonetheless.

"When I was young, I think." Tears roll down her rosy cheeks, and she daintily blows into her lace kerchief.

I spit back a retort. "Wasn't that before the war even started?"

"Yes, I suppose so." She fluffs her kerchief and buries her nose in it, emitting a rather unladylike honk.

If I weren't already so annoyed, I would've needled Betsy about her blatant breach of etiquette. Due to her prim deportment, such opportunities are rare and must be celebrated. "Well, then why are you weeping over a stranger?" I certainly hope that I don't act like this when I turn sixteen. This is such foolishness!

"I've lost hope, that's why! I'm afraid there won't be anyone left to marry by the time this horrid war ends." She lets out a loud wail and bursts into a fresh round of tears, gesturing toward a somber knot of widows.

I can't resist scolding her. "Hush, Betsy! You're only crying for yourself. Everyone else is here because they're sad for Joseph and his family. Since you're only sad for yourself, you should've stayed home and hosted your own pity party there!"

Betsy glares at me with flared nostrils. Turning her back, she crosses her arms with a flourish and tilts her nose in the air. Of course, I'm just as guilty. But at least I actually knew Joseph before the war! More importantly, he asked about me several times recently. And he was Stith's best friend. Stith. Losing Joseph must be devastating for him. I pray this won't break his spirit. The war has tested him for far too long.

Grabbing Penny, I sidle toward a band of men huddled together. Their conversation has got to be more compelling than Betsy moaning about her pitiful dearth of suitors. I sigh, wishing I could actually join the group. Alas, I must settle for what I can overhear. The next issue of *The Gazette* isn't due for another week, so any news is precious. Perhaps someone has a nugget to share.

Thankfully, the men are too engrossed in their discussion to notice us, and Penny and I exchange sly smiles. It's a success, at least for the moment!

A tall older man declares, "Aye, another attack is as inevitable as cicadas. Arnold will show up just when we've forgotten about him, just you see. He's biding his time. General Washington thinks he'll be back soon, so that's enough for me! He called it right back in January, but Governor Jefferson refused to call out our militia."

A deep voice pipes up from the back. "But now Lafayette's here to protect us! Once he captures Arnold, the Redcoats won't be calling him 'the Boy' no more!"

A third man snickers. "They are going to rue the day the Boy makes mincemeat out of them!"

I spy Mistress Blandford just across the way with a wistful look on her tear-streaked face. She's rubbing the locket containing Joseph's miniature portrait and hair snippet. The throngs of well-wishers no longer surround her. She's alone now. The poor woman looks like she hasn't slept since receiving the devastating news. To my shame, I still haven't spoken to her since that fateful day. Needless to say, I dread facing her. I know it's the right thing to do, but I fear uttering something foolish. Everything that comes to mind seems either excessively sorrowful or far too chipper.

Guilt soon gets the better of me. Taking a deep breath, I walk toward Mistress Blandford who reaches out in a tender embrace. I'm not sure how to react to her undeserved kindness. This woman could have become such a splendid mother-in-law. An uncomfortable silence follows, but then Mistress Bland-ford laces her arm through mine. The smooth enamel of her black mourning ring grazes my wrist like a caress, putting me at ease.

Mistress Blandford musters a tight-lipped smile, as if defying her wet cheeks and red-rimmed eyes. "Thank you for coming today, my dear. This certainly can't be easy for you either. I only wish our dear Joseph's body was here with us for a proper burial. I just can't bear to think of him dumped into a mass grave." Battling back tears, she fondles her locket once again. "I've had such nightmares of butchered boys piled in together and left to rot."

Before I realize what's happening, a torrent of tears rolls down my face. It comes as a welcome relief. At long last I'm mourning her loss, not my own.

"Mistress Blandford, please know that Stith would've done everything in his power to give Joseph a proper burial. I have no doubt he did the best he possibly could."

She nods, trying to find solace in my words. Within moments, though, she releases a high-pitched wail and then bites down hard on her lower lip.

"How? How did it ever come to this? It's not right! We have no son, no body, and we don't even have a church to mourn him in!" Her voice rises a pitch, bordering on hysteria. "Blandford Church was named for our family over fifty years ago. Jospeh's father was a vestryman there, and his grandfather before him! But how could we possibly hold his funeral there? It's Anglican! The head of the Anglican Church is the King, and it's the King's men who murdered our boy in cold blood. Oh, we've lost it all in this war — our sons, our church, our wealth, and our very happiness!"

Clutching a hand to her chest, Mistress Blandford winces as if in physical pain. "My apologies, my dear. My only comfort is that Joseph and his brother are now reunited in heaven. Soon we will join them there for all eternity. I must cling to that, or I shall go mad. King George has stolen my two precious boys, but he cannot have my sanity as well." She stamps her foot. "I dare say he may not! Let *him* go mad, not me!" Her intensity is so out of character. Without realizing it, I step backward.

"Oh my dear, did I startle you? Please excuse me for my outburst." With a long face, she fishes around in her pocket, opens my fist, and folds a shiny gold ring into it. "Well, it just wasn't meant to be, was it? I had so hoped that Joseph would give you this ring. Since I have only a daughter left, though, it belongs to you now."

Louise ambles up, her long blond braids askew. She laces her arms around her mother's waist. A shy smile crosses her freckled face. "He was so very sweet on you, Miss Susanna. I heard it myself! Every night Mama sits by the fire and reads his letters to us."

My eyes blur with tears once again. Perhaps Joseph would've been the perfect husband, the love of my life even. Well, now I'll never know. Everyone's life is on hold until this dreadful war ends. That's presuming we're fortunate enough to emerge from it alive. As usual, there's nothing to do but wait, hope, and pray.

When we set out for home, the sun is setting. As if on cue, the sinister skies finally open up and release a downpour. Chilly plump raindrops splatter all over me. Within seconds I'm drenched to the bone despite the heat.

As we approach the Fredericks' farm, my heart races. The closer we get, the faster it pounds. Under my breath, I vow, "I shan't remain quiet this time, I shan't!" Much to my relief, however, no one awaits us. I keep my eyes downcast for a different reason entirely. It's vanity. I can't stop ogling my new ring from Mistress Blandford. I certainly don't deserve such a lavish gift, or any gift at all for that matter. But its golden gleam dazzles me nonetheless.

One thing is certain, however unsettling. Another funeral feast will take place somewhere nearby soon. But no one knows where, or for whom. I shiver at the thought of hosting one at Bollingbrook. Despite the loss of Mary and her baby, we Bollings are long overdue a casualty of war. Of course, that presumes the Grim Reaper operates by a code of fairness, the ultimate fallacy. Death follows no rules at all.

Mother and I are so fortunate that we haven't suffered such a misfortune. However, for me the most frightening part is my inability to prevent something horrible from happening to Stith. If only I could aid our cause somehow, then perhaps I could make a difference, despite my flaws. But that's not to be; not for a mere girl anyway. Although it pains me, I must resolve to do what I can at home. There's no point in focusing my energy on what lies beyond my reach.

If my place is at Bollingbrook, I must accept that. Even more, I must embrace my role here. That means no more complaining, daydreaming, eavesdropping, or gossiping! Clothing our threadbare Continental Army is my only way to assist, so that's what I must do. After all, how can an army fight when practically naked? By helping to make our upcoming bee the most productive yet, I'll make a real contribution to outfit our brave soldiers. And there's an additional bonus. If I win my age group, *The Gazette* will print my name in its next issue! However, that requires me to outperform Betsy. That's highly unlikely, but I must try.

CHAPTER 8
MOTHER'S SPINNING BEE

At last, the long-anticipated day of the spinning bee arrives. I've been in the summer kitchen since before sunrise, so I'm quite bleary-eyed. Thankfully the roaring fireplaces have lit up the room. Auntie Ruth scurries around with her wooden spoon, stirring the boiling cauldrons of Liberty tea. Her weary eyes are drooping far more than usual. I suspect she has worked all night long. Now she's adding even more basil leaves from her kitchen garden. I savor its pungent yet sweet aroma as it overpowers the room. Nowadays I can't even remember what real tea tastes like anymore.

Mother barks out orders, orchestrating the last-minute details. "Sukey and Penny, please get the wagon and start loading it." Then she whispers to me, "I worry about Auntie Ruth carrying anything these days. She's far older than me, and I feel ancient enough as it is." Mother chuckles and flashes a rare smile.

As we're heading to the stable, Leroy runs up and blocks my path with his flailing arms. "Miss Sukey, I seen something!" His eyes dart every which way, wild and unfocused. "I seen some boats coming upriver!"

Penny walks ahead and disappears into the stable.

Try as I might to be kind, my words come out clipped. "What do you mean, Leroy?" Itching to depart, I have no patience for his shenanigans. Even if he's telling the truth, he's probably confused. Tobacco can only grow for four years in the same soil. So every winter Big Hank expands the planting area further away from the river. Leroy has been working way out in those newly cleared fields, so he doesn't know boats come upriver all day long.

"Redcoat boats. That's what I seen. I know it." There's an edge of anger to his voice that makes me bristle. He's adamant to the point of insolence.

My eyes narrow into slits. "Are you sure? How do you know they're Redcoats?" I make no attempt to hide my doubt or annoyance. He probably just wants some attention.

With bulging eyes, Leroy is insistent. "I seen big cannons up front. They weren't no fishing boats. No, ma'am! They gunboats! And I seen red uniforms."

I'm still not convinced. If Big Hank doesn't trust him, I sure don't either. "Well, surely someone would've warned us if they made it all the way up the Appomattox."

His voice grows raw. "You don't believe me, Miss Sukey. But I'm telling you, I be speaking the truth. I seen it with my own eyes, clear as day."

I groan. I'm at my wits' end. Soon it'll be time to set off for the bee, and Penny still hasn't emerged. I have no doubt she's avoiding Leroy. "Well, who else saw this? Was anyone else with you?"

"No, just me." Hanging his head, he mumbles, "I was late this morning, so Big Hank sent me off to weed on the river." Suddenly, he bolts forward, thrusting his head into the stable.

"Penny, you hiding in there? I know you don't believe me neither!"

After an awkward silence, Penny finally leads the carriage out. She looks straight at him but doesn't say a word.

He speaks in a low voice, close to a growl. "So you got nothing to say? You always picking them over your own brother!"

Her facial muscles harden and her eyes grow steely. "Leroy, I ain't taking nobody's side, but I ain't getting all riled up about some darn ship you seen out there neither."

I don't have time for his nonsense, but I also want to defuse the situation for Penny's sake. "Leroy, we believe you. Of course we do. But we've got to finish getting ready. We're already running late. I'll talk to Mother later on, I promise. Perhaps you did see a scout of some sort. Lord knows there are plenty of them out there."

As we walk the carriage over to the summer kitchen, he hollers after us. "Miz Susanna, I done seen it. I swear it, Penny!"

"Why does he have to drag me into this? I always tell him, just get on with your work!" Penny shakes her head. "I'm not sure if I believe him." We sink into a tense silence.

Once we are finally on the way, Mother chatters like a giddy girl. I don't dare threaten her pleasant mood with Leroy's dubious sighting. "Our usual ladies will be there, so it should be a lively crowd once again. And there's other good news to share! Speaker Harrison arranged for a carriage to bring Mistress Harrison and the children over from Berkeley." She turns to look at me. "Remember, Sukey, this is their first real outing since Arnold's treachery, so please be especially gentle with them." I want to bristle, but instead I hold my tongue. Of course I'd welcome them with good will, without any need for prodding!

Mother continues. "They're still quite fragile after January.

How provident that Speaker Harrison noticed the Redcoats entering the plantation." She makes a clucking sound. "It's a wonder they escaped with the clothes on their backs." After a pause, she shakes her head. "My heart goes out to the poor servants those marauders dragged off."

I nod, trying to envision the terror they must have felt. It boggles my mind. There is sadness everywhere these days. No one is immune.

Mother murmurs, "I'm not sure if Rebecca will attend today. She's not doing well, not well at all." She purses her lips. "Oh, I can only imagine the ache in her heart right now. She's as fragile as a newborn babe, the poor dear. As hard as it may be, it would do her such good to get out, even if just to air out her grief. We all know a bee isn't just a social occasion, although we do certainly enjoy ourselves, don't we?" Mother doesn't wait for a response. "Even Mistress Higgins couldn't accuse Rebecca of abandoning her mourning too soon."

The thought of Mistress Blandford still makes me queasy. I finally hid the gold ring deep in the straw ticking of my mattress. It was a generous gift that I surely didn't deserve.

Big Hank and a throng of slaves plod along behind us. A second wagon follows, loaded with the spinning wheels, fresh wool, and raw fibers already prepared for spinning, along with baskets of food and Liberty tea. The women will clean the fresh wool and card it, using wooden brushes to separate the fibers. Then Mother and I will spin our wooden wheels to pull the fibers into thread. Later, back at home, we'll have the servants weave it into fabric out in the loom house. And that's when the real monotony begins. Mother and I will gather by the fireplace for hours on end to sew uniforms for our brave soldiers, one agonizing stitch after another. Try as I might, I don't do it well. I have plenty of revolting scabs on my fingertips to prove it.

Basking in the early-morning sunshine, Mother, Mistress

Bland, and I set up our wheels and stools on the flattest spot we can find at the center of Petersburg Square. Right away, Mistress Bland gushes about her new stallion, barely stopping to take a breath.

"Oh, what a gorgeous creature he is, rippling with muscles. What a sweet colt, but quite skittish from what I can tell. He's black all over, so I've named him Raven."

Mother doesn't even pretend to pay a speck of attention to her cousin. Instead she looks the other way, observing the other ladies trickling in. I'm even less interested in Mistress Bland's chatter and let out a heavy sigh. She reminds me of Betsy carrying on about Peter Francisco, but at least Betsy is obsessed with a human being.

I'm determined to concentrate on spinning today, hoping to win the contest despite the odds against me. If Betsy prevails again, I won't be able to bear her crowing about it. I haven't even caught a glimpse of her yet, and she's already annoyed me. That cousin of mine has the uncanny ability to get under my skin and stay there, just like ringworms. Now I'm irritated with myself. On the bright side, at least another victory for her would prevent her babbling about her only topic of conversation. I chuckle under my breath.

I force myself to change my attitude. The slight breeze, along with plenty of lemony sunshine, is surely an omen for the most productive bee ever! A swarm of ladies, young and old, now fills the square, all chattering away. The young boys and slaves follow behind, balancing wheels on their shoulders. In their hands they also carry rough-hewn baskets brimming with fibers for spinning. By the time the late-afternoon shadows appear on the square, we plan to have hundreds upon hundreds of skeins of thread and wool. We even hope to set a new record! I'm feeling like quite a Petticoat Patriot now!

Betsy and Aunt Sarah stroll onto the square, and I scowl.

Desperately, I scan the crowd, hoping that someone, anyone, will come sit next to me fast. I'd be content with just about anyone other than sour Mistress Higgins. Much to my dismay, this is not to be. Betsy and her mother plunk their wheels and stools down within inches of mine. In their dithering, they fail to notice the uneven cobblestones, so I snicker to myself as Betsy's wheel wobbles and then topples over with a clatter, knocking over Aunt Sarah's and mine in the process. Betsy lets out an exaggerated huff.

"Settle yourself, cousin," I mutter, stifling a giggle. I resist the strong temptation to scold her. Of course, I can well imagine her scathing reaction had I been the clumsy one, which is usually the case.

Flustered, Betsy glares at me as if it was my fault. She rights her wheel and then her mother's. Ignoring mine, she leaves it lying in a heap.

"Oh, if it weren't for this dreadful war, I'd have a cluster of handsome lads fighting to set this up for me."

Aunt Sarah chimes in, her voice sweet and soothing. "And you certainly would, too, darling. You're the loveliest girl here." I want to retch. As an afterthought, she glances over at me. "And of course, you too, Susanna."

I roll my eyes and right my wheel as Mother shoots me a sharp look. I sigh, knowing she's forbidden me to make a saucy retort, however well deserved. Adopting a false sense of cheer, I oblige her.

"Why, what a glorious day! God is surely smiling down on His Daughters of Liberty today."

Thankfully Mistress Harrison arrives with her younger children in tow. They cling to her full skirts as if they're afraid to lose sight of her for a second. They scan the animated crowd, their eyes wide with suspicion. Eventually she is able to settle them down on a blanket behind her to embroider their alphabet samplers. A somber Mistress Blandford and

Louise are among the last to arrive. Much to Mother's delight, they set up right behind us. When Louise gives my braid a playful tug, I turn and chat with her.

Mother waves her hands in the air and calls the group to order. "Ladies! My fellow Sisters of Liberty! Welcome to our first spinning bee of the spring season. What a gorgeous day! It's such an honor to gather with you again to support our mighty cause. Remember, this thread and yarn will help clothe our beloved soldiers who want for absolutely everything. Every inch we can spin will bolster our troops and propel us toward victory."

The ladies burst into a resounding round of applause. Mother pauses and looks around the group, ensuring she has their rapt attention.

"So, here's our plan for the day! As usual, we shall spin for the morning and then enjoy a picnic here on the square at high noon. My servants will provide Liberty tea made with fresh basil from Bollingbrook. Please help yourself to a cup or two before it disappears. This afternoon, we will have our contests and recognize our most productive members. Then we shall spin again for the duration. Let's work hard; we're clothing our own! Remember to measure your thread along the way, and to keep track of how many skeins you've produced. *The Gazette* will publish our grand total, so we hope to break our previous record! Let the spinning commence!"

With the bee officially underway, the ladies press their feet down on their treadles. Immediately a thunderous noise fills the air. It's a bizarre combination of whirring of the large wheels and the buzzing of the smaller ones. In addition, there are a variety of other creaks, squeaks, and rattles. At the back of the crowd, the slaves toil over mounds of flax and freshly shorn wool to prepare it for spinning. It's a tedious process. First they pluck out clumps of dirt, smooth over the lumps, and loosen up the fibers. Then others use wooden paddles lined with bristles to card the teased fibers and straighten them.

Despite the noise, the women chatter among themselves, adding the gentle hum of their conversations to the cacophony. Mistress Harrison looks over each shoulder and then hisses to Mother, "We're still terrified he's going to send them back. Every day I wake with dread in my heart, wondering if this will be the day."

Of course, I know she's referring to the slaves that Arnold stole from them, but I still don't understand. "But ma'am, don't you want them to come home?"

Apparently my voice was too loud because she shushes me. Then she leans toward me and speaks just above a whisper. "I don't want my maid Ursula to hear. You see, she lost her entire family. She was helping me dress at the time, so she was the only one we could save." She narrows her eyes, and her voice drips with bitterness. "Unfortunately, Cornwallis makes a habit of turning our slaves as weapons against us, and deadly ones at that. You see, he infects them with the pox. Then he waits until they're good and sick." Her eyes lock onto mine. "And finally, out of the goodness of his heart, he sends them back to spread the disease to us."

Repulsed, I thrust myself back on my stool, nearly losing my balance. How unbelievably cruel, even for Redcoats! Mother makes regretful clucking sounds and shakes her head.

Leroy and some of the other slaves make their way onto the square, lugging the huge tubs of tea. He makes a beeline over to Mother and drops his down on the bricks with a sharp clang. Pausing to catch his breath, he wipes his sweaty forehead with his sleeve. "Mistis, here be some tea for you ladies." Mother nods but doesn't look at him. Instead she bends over, installing a new bobbin on her spindle.

He waits for a few seconds, but she doesn't acknowledge him. He continues, "Ma'am, I got to tell you something mighty important. When I was working in the fields earlier, I done seen some ships come downriver like I ain't never seen before. They done gave me a fright."

Mother still looks down, now adjusting the tension on her wheel. "Thank you for telling me, Leroy." Her voice is flat.

"Yes, ma'am. But I's speaking the truth. I seen some boats with big canons up front."

Mistress Harrison scoffs as she picks at her pile of flax to spin. "We just crossed the river from our Berkeley, and I didn't see anything out of the ordinary." She glares up at Leroy. "Perhaps you've had a bit too much sun. Of course, I don't believe we've seen the last of Arnold, but I can't imagine he'd arrive in broad daylight. Unfortunately for us, he's too clever an officer for that."

Leroy's eyes stretch wide. "Yes'm, but I seen what I seen. I swear they was there. And they warn't no ships. They was gunboats."

Mother interjects. "As I said, Leroy, thank you. Now let's not cause any unnecessary alarm, shall we?" She frowns and raises her eyebrows toward the Harrison children who are engrossed in their work. She waves a hand, dismissing him. "You'd best set up the station for the Liberty tea now."

Leroy shakes his head and frowns. With a grunt, he picks up the massive container and marches off.

Mistress Harrison sniffs. "Well, we certainly don't see Mary Willing Byrd here today, do we? I dare say her poor husband must be rolling in his grave right now." She gestures to the substantial group. "I don't care who here disagrees with me. If she won't help us, not even once, she's definitely no Daughter of Liberty. And if she isn't with us, she's against us. It doesn't matter if she's quiet about it. After all, she gave Arnold safe harbor during the January raid. She'll gladly do it again. Mark my words!"

Mother gives a sharp nod and raises her eyebrows. "You'll

find no disagreement from me. Her Tory sympathies are quite obvious to anyone not busy looking the other way."

With a glance back at her children, Mistress Harrison lowers her voice to a hiss. "Since my husband had the privilege of signing the Declaration, Arnold has had his revenge. He made quite a roaring bonfire of our possessions. Our families spent their lifetimes collecting that artwork and furniture." Mistress Harrison fingers the portrait miniature hanging from her neck. "This is the only portrait that survived the plunder, only because I was wearing it. How I hope to God he falls headfirst into his next inferno, the swine! He made off with everything else – our slaves, horses, and every bit of food. He spared only our bed and the house itself, saving it for himself at the war's end, no doubt. Good God! They'd have to draw and quarter me before I'd allow such a travesty to take place!" A cloud of rage covers her drawn face. I can't help cringing. I've never seen an angrier human being.

"As for his dear cousin-in-law, Mary Willing Byrd, he took from her at Westover, too, of course. He made off with slaves, horses, and even ferryboats. But he left everything else undisturbed *and* promised her compensation. There's a reason for that! She's a Tory sympathizer through and through!"

Mistress Higgins throws up her hands. "Well, surely this can be no surprise! What do you expect? Arnold's wife is her first cousin after all! Lord knows that meddling Peggy Shippen from Philadelphia is as Tory as they come. No doubt she did her very best to poison him against our cause. However, that doesn't excuse the louse one bit. How I long to catch Arnold myself and collect that 5,000 guinea bounty!" She chortles. "Then Lafayette could hang him, just as General Washington ordered."

With a mischievous twinkle in her eye, Mistress Harrison

pipes in. "And I dare say Berkeley would provide the perfect setting, right on the ashes of his bonfire!"

Mother smiles. "Now that would be a sight to behold. I dare say our Lafayette would take great pleasure in that!"

Betsy interjects. "Why, ladies, look at this handsome Continental uniform I made myself from start to finish!" With a coy smile, she holds up her impressive handiwork. "I spun the thread at the last bee with you all, then wove it on my loom, and sewed it myself. Might I say, it is ever so lovely." She giggles. "I am feeling quite patriotic right now." She adjusts the tag sewn into the collar and pats it down. Of course, she's sewn her name there in a flowery script, a symbol of female support from home.

Although I want to throttle her, I settle for a simple chiding. "Your boasting is most insufferable. We're all making contributions as best we can."

In a sing-song manner, Betsy croons her retort. "Say all you want, cousin, but perhaps the handsome soldier who wears this will come find me! But oh, fickle me! I do find the French uniform so dashing as well. How marvelous would it be to have a Frenchman court me and even propose!" She puts her hands to her flushed cheeks.

Much to my disgust, her annoying reverie continues. "I would start a whole new life in Paris wearing all the latest fashions! Perhaps Louis XVI and Queen Marie Antoinette would invite me to court from time to time. Oh, it sounds like a delicious dream, doesn't it? And there's no dreadful revolution over in France to muddle things up like here. It's a shame General Lafayette is already married to a cousin of the King." She lets out an exaggerated sigh. "After all, he's one of the richest men in all of Europe! But I believe his aide-de-camp, Colonel Gimat, remains eligible." She bursts into a giggle.

I'm unable to contain my irritation a moment longer and

lash out at her. "Oh, quit your mooning, you ninny. It sounds like a silly dream because it is a silly dream! We're here to support our cause, not plot how to snare a husband from the French aristocracy."

Betsy shakes her head back and forth like a wise old woman. "Say what you will, cousin, but you will soon be sorely in need of a husband. And I dare say your churlish personality will only make it more difficult for you." She shakes her head, feigning pity for my bleak marriage prospects.

Mother raises her eyebrows and gives me a pointed look, warning me not to respond. Smoldering, I roll my eyes, but I'm even more determined. I absolutely must triumph over Betsy today.

I look up as the town crier makes his way through the crowded square. My foot falls off the treadle, and I gasp. This is not a social call. He's clad in his official regalia, a red and gold jacket over a white ruffled blouse with the traditional livery colors of red, black, and gold. The usual jaunty feathers stand atop his tricorne hat.

Stricken with worry, I look around the square for clues. Good Lord, something awful must have happened. It must be of great importance to interrupt the spinning bee!

Squire Matthews takes long strides and swings his hand bell as he bellows, "Oyez! Oyez!" Chills run down my spine.

Within seconds the spinning wheels cease their thundering. Utter silence blankets the square like an unexpected blizzard. The crowd watches with drawn faces as he arrives in the center of the square. After a perfunctory nod to Mother, he opens his handbill with a flourish. Then he scans the crowd, ensuring everyone's undivided attention, and barks out his message. "This is a call to arms! Within the hour, Benedict Arnold has landed at Westover Plantation on the north bank of the James for a second time. A barrage of enemy cannons announced his arrival, and more warships with many Redcoats are imminent. Prince George County hereby mobilizes the members of its militia immediately! A messenger has been dispatched to inform the General Assembly in Richmond and General Lafayette at his undisclosed location north of here. Ladies, prepare yourselves for an immediate raid on Petersburg!" Marching over to the nearest pole, he fishes a thorn from his waist pocket, posts the handbill, and stomps off.

Everyone remains frozen in place for a few seconds. Then Harriet lets out a fearsome howl, prompting screams to erupt all over the square. Every fiber of my being tempts me to join in. With an ashen face, Mother rises from her seat, struggling to maintain her composure. Cupping her hands around her mouth, she tries to shout above the din that only grows louder. "Ladies, ladies! Please, there's no need to panic. I'm sure Mistress Byrd is steeping a lovely cup of tea for Arnold right now. We Patriots have always been like little David fighting the giant Goliath. This time shall be no different!" Alas, her valiant attempt to calm the crowd is in vain; utter chaos has overtaken the group. It's hard to believe we were working with such diligence just a few minutes ago.

The crowd scatters in every direction, trampling everything in its path, including the toppled piles of rough flax and wool. Some older men race over to the town crier in a feeble attempt to press for more information. Frightened by the sudden commotion, the small children fill the air with their high-pitched screams and sobs. The ladies jump up from their seats, not even noticing that they've knocked over wheels and baskets in their haste. They shriek a litany of orders to their beleaguered slaves who snatch up every belonging they can possibly hold and hustle toward the carriages. The Negroes soon fall behind, moaning as they try to keep pace despite their overflowing armloads of gear.

Beating drums now punctuate the air. In front of the Golden Ball Tavern, a young boy tugs on a long rope, clanging the massive brass bell summoning all the able men to arms. Just down the way, the bell at James Durrell's Tavern rings as well.

Mother mutters, "Calling up the Virginia militia, are they? What militia? Why do they even bother? They're all down in Guilford Courthouse, half of them below ground. And let's not forget the other 1,400 Virginians who are still prisoners down in Charleston!"

A tingling sensation creeps up the back of my neck. With that one announcement, our sleepy village has become a dangerous battleground with no one here to defend us. I pray my brothers won't learn of Arnold's invasion until it's long over. Knowing their home is under siege but not being here to defend it would torture them. Of course, that's presuming they're still alive.

Mistress Harrison's face is drained of color as she speaks in a weak voice. "So that slave boy of yours was right after all. The British have arrived back at Westover, unfortunately next door to our beloved Berkeley again. And you are correct as well. We have no one left here to protect us."

Mother responds in a crisp tone. "Well, we do have our Prince George County militia, however small that may be. Major General Von Steuben has been their drillmaster for months now. Let's not forget that dreadful winter in Valley Forge when he transformed those freezing boys into fine Continental soldiers. Surely he'll lead ours in making a respectable stand. We can't ask for more than that." She continues in a smaller voice. "Even though they are completely outnumbered and pitifully ill-equipped."

Looking faint, Mistress Harrison lifts a hand to her heaving chest. "Heavens, I just recalled my Benjamin is in the county militia too! He considered it his duty as Speaker, of course. We never thought it'd amount to anything."

Mother snaps back at her, "Elizabeth! Of course Petersburg's a target! It's the main stopover for troops moving between north and south."

Mistress Harrison's cheeks redden. "Well, Susanna, there was no fighting in Virginia until that arch traitor arrived." She huffs. "No doubt my Benjamin would insist on playing his part, but thankfully he's up with the House of Burgesses. Hopefully this will be all over by the time he can return."

Mother replies, "No doubt it will. He's too shrewd a man to come before it's safe. Arnold would have a noose around his neck in no time."

Mistress Harrison pulls up her shoulders as if a lightning bolt has struck her. "Regardless, we must leave at once! Arnold may lay waste to Berkeley this time, but I won't allow my children to smell the smoke. After all, my dear William Henry is only eight, and nightmares have plagued both him and Sarah since January." Her voice quavers. "Well, Arnold can't hurt me anymore, short of murdering my family. Save for that, nothing is worse than losing every portrait, our entire ancestry." Her eyes well with tears as she grips the portrait miniature locket around her neck.

Mother gently touches her shoulder. "Please come stay at Bollingbrook, all of you, until Benjamin arrives."

"You can't be serious!" Mistress Harrison gasps. "We can't go back there! It's most unsafe!" Stricken, she puts a hand to her chest. "My children and I will not stay in the zone of danger, not after we have already barely escaped with our lives. Their lives are far too precious to put at risk! I won't allow Arnold the opportunity to capture the family of Virginia's Speaker and the only Signer along the James."

William Henry lets out a wail, wraps his thin arms around her waist, and buries his face in her embroidered gown.

Stroking his hair, she declares, "I intend for my son to become a distinguished soldier someday. And perhaps he'll lead Virginia, or even our great country, if his older brothers don't beat him to it." She shakes her head with great fervor. "No, we shall head west immediately."

"Do as you will, but we shall not flee." Mother's tone is resolute as she folds her arms in a decided manner. "This is our land and our country, and this is where we will remain, Arnold, or no Arnold." She snorts. "Of course, it comes as no surprise. We knew he would be on the prowl again soon, what with the British Navy at his disposal. He knows full well how dismal ours is."

Mother's brazen attitude bewilders me. After all, Mistress Harrison is speaking reason considering her traumatic experience. As my legs quiver, I want to evacuate City Point with every breath in my body. There's no need to expose ourselves to such danger when we could leave until the raid is over.

"Suit yourself, Susanna. We shall find others heading west then. Come along, children." With a curt nod, Mistress Harrison marches off with the sniffling William Henry still affixed to her waist and a dazed Sarah trailing behind. Her wild-eyed maid Ursula shuffles along behind her, weighed down with belongings as tears pour down her face.

Within minutes, my desire to distinguish myself as a Revolutionary heroine has evaporated. All I want to do is run off willy-nilly with the Harrisons. If that exposes me as chicken-hearted, then so be it. I shudder; at least I'd be a safe coward then. I know any efforts to convince Mother will come to no avail, though; she won't tolerate any such tommy-rot. For Mother, weakness is never an acceptable option.

Of course, Mother has already devised a plan. "Big Hank, round up the servants and bring them all back to Bolling-brook right away. Then gather the men and boys, and head over to the warehouses with every sack and shovel you can find. I need you to secure them as best you can. Sukey and I will finish gathering up everything here and meet you over there." Mother's mouth is set in a grim line. "If Arnold does invade, he's sure to come after our tobacco, just like in Richmond."

Big Hank's eyes are somber. "Yes, ma'am." He gives her a respectful nod. "I bring everyone in from planting soon as I get there."

"We'll need every last one of them. Of course, we don't have much for supplies, but you'll have to make do as best you can."

I'm in a stupor of denial; I can't believe this is really happening. The loathsome Arnold and his British Regulars are just across the river, poised to attack, and General Lafayette and his troops aren't anywhere in the vicinity. It's the stuff of nightmares. If only I could pinch myself and wake up from this horror!

Wicker baskets still overflowing with crockery lie scattered about and overturned; spinning equipment lies abandoned all over the square, even costly wheels and distaffs. "We shall gather up every last belonging and return it all later. We shan't hurry ourselves, not for those arrogant brutes!" With jerking movements, Mother stoops over and picks up several discarded items.

I look on, battling a rising sense of panic. With a deep breath, I resign myself to the task at hand, insane as it is. I haul the first vat of tea back to the wagon, stopping with each lurching step to catch my breath. I can't help wishing Mother had ordered Leroy to stay and help us. Plus, I need to apologize for rebuffing him this morning. After all, he was absolutely right. There's no longer any doubt about that.

Even after we've loaded the carriage with every last scrap, Mother remains undeterred. "Now, before heading home, we shall go to Bolling's Point to see about the warehouses. They must be as secure as possible. Last year's crop for every planter in Tidewater is at stake! We owe them our very best efforts to save them."

Crestfallen, I crave the comfort of Bollingbrook even if it's an illusion. From the distance come ominous rumbling sounds. My mind races ahead. Perhaps the British troops are advancing already. Knowing my voice will surely tremble, I don't dare ask Mother if she hears it too. Above all, she mustn't know how scared I am. It would crush her to find out her daughter is a coward, but I'm not sure how much longer I can hide it.

CHAPTER 9
A PERPLEXING ACQUAINTANCE

When we arrive, the wharf is enveloped in an eerie silence. With a drawn face, Mother marches down the wooden planks, oblivious as they creak out a discordant symphony. With military precision, she checks each warehouse door, making occasional tsking sounds and muttering under her breath.

Discouraged, I sink onto a weatherbeaten bench; I can't make any sense of it. Mother can try all she wants, but she can't prevent Arnold from destroying the whole lot of them. If he wants to burn the tobacco, he will. Unfortunately it's no more complicated than that.

A scruffy Negro man emerges from the other end of the wharf, shuffling along as he counts the warehouses. Laying eyes on Mother, he stops dead in his tracks and stares at her. Then he breaks into a holler.

"Ma'am, this ain't no place for a lady, not now!"

"Sakes alive, who are you?" Arching her back, she puts her hands on her hips and takes long strides toward him. "Come here, and stop with your shouting! Pray tell, where is your master?"

The Negro approaches Mother, studying her as he strokes his shaggy beard. "I used to have me a master over in New Kent County, but I done run off." He smirks, revealing a mouthful of stained teeth with sizable gaps between them. "Now I've got a new one of my own choice, General Benedict Arnold." He yanks his sagging trousers up and stands taller, impervious to Mother's narrowed eyes. "I'm in His Majesty's Service now, and a free man once this war be done."

Noting Mother's scowl and upturned nose, the Negro snickers. "Ma'am, if you with the rebels, you best get out of here and take your pretty girl home with you."

I hope she will heed his sage advice, but I know better. It will take far more than an insolent runaway to intimidate my fearless mother.

She stares down her nose at him. "You are correct; I do not support your King." She purses her lips. "However, as you may not be aware, these warehouses are my property. If you are truly a Redcoat, as you claim, then why are you here by yourself, away from the rest? And where is your uniform?" She raises her eyebrows, glaring at his tattered and stained smock. "Perhaps you're just another runaway trying to avoid capture."

Without flinching, he stares back at her and responds in a low gravelly voice. "Ma'am, trust me, you ain't got time for the likes of me. You don't want to get caught down here, or that girl of yours either." He shakes his head. "No, ma'am! This battle sure ain't going to last too long with all those Regulars coming onto the shore. Before you know it, there'll be a huge mob down here tonight with torches lit."

Mother all but hisses, "What battle?" She tilts her head. "How do you know so much?"

Despite the deserted area, he peeks over his shoulder and drops his voice to a whisper. "Look, ma'am, I'm trying to help you, you see. I could get myself shot for this, but I'm the scout for General Arnold. He don't know these parts, but I sure do. He's from up there in Connecticut. I'm showing him around here later on after the battle. He wants to see them buildings here for himself." He makes a sweeping gesture toward the warehouses, thrusts his face forward, and locks eyes with her. "You must leave now!"

Mother's eyes widen; I can tell she's starting to believe him. I just pray she heeds his advice.

"For the love of God, don't let him burn them! My daughter and I are the only ones left, and it's our only livelihood!" Much to my surprise, her voice catches.

Is she stifling a sob? I'm flabbergasted; I've never seen Mother so close to begging, let alone to a Negro.

"Ma'am, there's only one way General Arnold ain't going to burn your warehouses, and you sure ain't going to like it." He shakes his head, but a glimmer of hope shines on Mother's face.

I know what she's thinking. Perhaps she can still save last year's tobacco harvest after all!

"Go on," Mother prods. She leans forward within inches of his unshaven face, yellowed teeth, and presumably foul-smelling breath.

He hesitates and then shakes his head again as if already anticipating her reaction. Finally he takes in a deep breath and spits it out. "You've got to put the tobacco out into the street, so he can load it right onto them ships." He looks sheepish. "And that's the only way he ain't going to mess with them warehouses of yours."

The fleeting promise vanishes from Mother's face as it darkens like a massive storm on the horizon.

The Negro strokes his mangy beard again. "I said you weren't going to like it." So the Redcoats would spare the warehouses themselves if Mother forfeited the tobacco to the

King! Of course, a warehouse without its contents is a useless shell, like an eggshell without its yolk inside.

"Absolutely not!" Mother stamps her foot. "I'll have you know Arnold offered the same in Richmond, to spare the city from burning if they gave up their tobacco. Our brave Governor Jefferson immediately said no then, and so do I now." She gives a deep nod. "You can go ahead and torch it all now for all I care." Turning on her heel, she storms off.

I'm dumbfounded.

The Negro growls at Mother's retreating back, "I be warning you, ma'am. This place ain't safe, not for long. Those King's men ain't seen pretty ladies in a right long time. Every minute you stay down here, you're risking it all."

I shiver. Surely even Mother will see reason now.

At long last she relents with a defeated sigh. After turning for a last regretful look at the warehouses, Mother marches toward the carriage.

Wanting to scream with relief, I am right on her heels lest she change her mind.

The man glances over his shoulder for a second time and hisses, "Ma'am, I got to go and so do you and your girl, but they know what's in that County Courthouse of yours. They coming for those munitions tomorrow morning first thing." He cocks his head. "It ain't no secret no more."

Mother turns to him and puts her hands on her hips. "Who are you anyway?" Her voice drips with skepticism. "You still haven't told me. What's your name? Presuming you have one, of course."

Panic flashes over his face as he blurts out, "I can't say no more." With that, he sprints up the ramp and disappears.

Baffled, I struggle to understand his motivation. "Mother, why would Arnold's guide want to help us Patriots, even a tiny bit? Especially protecting our supplies! Why would he want us to save them?"

Mother scratches her head. "Quite frankly, I have no earthly idea, Sukey. Well, we certainly must move everything out of the courthouse tonight, in case he speaks the truth." Her voice grows wary. "He seems to know an awful lot for a simple runaway."

I nod. He certainly does.

CHAPTER 10
ARNOLD'S RAID

Within minutes, Big Hank and a large group of male slaves arrive, bogged down with shovels, brooms, buckets, and hemp bags. Covered in sweat and dust, they hardly look capable of stopping the mighty British Army from doing anything. "Ma'am, I got all the men I could find right quick. We left a few stragglers behind, just in case you and Miss Sukey need something back there, but we ready to work and make these warehouses real tight."

Mother gulps as a flash of fear crosses her face. Like me, she hadn't contemplated the possibility of Redcoats arriving at Bollingbrook. Within seconds, though, her mask of composure returns.

"Thank you so much, Big Hank, but it's no use. Our tobacco is as good as gone." She shakes her head. "As it turns out, the militia is more in need of your help right now. Take your men and head over to the trading station. Tell Mister Jones I've sent you to move the military supplies from the County Courthouse over to Colonel Banister's estate, since Battersea is more heavily fortified." Then she murmurs, more to herself than anyone else, "It may be futile, but we must at least try."

At long last, we head toward the cocoon of home, and I can hardly contain my relief, however naïve. I hear more rumbling in the distance, but once again I question my over-active imagination and frayed nerves. Nevertheless the bells still clang without ceasing, beckoning all able-bodied men to assist in the defense.

Mother scoffs under her breath. "They can sound the alarm for days on end, but nobody else is going to answer their call. We haven't any whole young men left."

Once we're back at Bollingbrook, the ominous sound of Redcoats marching on Petersburg continues. With trembling hands and laborious breath, Harriet makes a valiant effort to dust the parlor while mumbling, "Lawd, have mercy." When she drops Mother's favorite vase, chipping its mouth, Mother bristles and orders her out to the summer kitchen to help Auntie Ruth.

Finally, even Mother has no choice but to acknowledge the movement of enemy troops in the distance. "So our invaders have come ashore and are making themselves at home, are they? It's such a pity General Lafayette isn't in the area with his troops. All we can do is wait and pray our militia will make an honorable stand and hold them off. They may be poorly trained and outnumbered, but we must have confidence that General Von Steuben and Colonel Banister shall do their very best. In the meantime we must stay productive. Now, let's head into the parlor for some spinning. As Proverbs says, 'Idle hands are the devil's workshop'. We can never have enough thread!"

Much to my chagrin, my hands shake too much to operate my wheel with any precision. The resulting thread is lumpy and bumpy, and therefore utterly useless. Even worse, I can barely breathe. Rather than admit my weakness to Mother, though, I continue on, hoping she doesn't check my progress or notice my ragged breath. Once she leaves the room, though, I switch to the much simpler task of carding wool. Yet even that I cannot do, so I work the same pile over and over again, trying to maintain a façade of busyness.

Despite the distance, I can soon make out high-pitched fifes and low-pitched drums that lead the soldiers onto the battlefield. Then the drummers play their beatings directing them into position. Finally the music directs them to load their muskets and fire. There is a barrage of popping sounds that evolves into heavy gunfire, punctuated by the boom of a cannon firing off. I'm amazed I can still make out both the instruments over the sounds of battle. Our windows settle into a constant rattle with an occasional jarring of the house to its foundation.

To escape, I retreat out back to the kitchen yard. However, the battle seems even closer there, giving me a worse fright. I scuttle back inside, feeling as jittery as Harriet, and confide in Penny.

"I've a mind to barricade myself down in the tunnel to escape this savage battle." But Mother mustn't know how frightened I really am, so I don't dare let on to her.

Each minute passes like a decade as we sit perched on the edge of our seats, startled by every sound of battle. Several terrifying hours eventually pass, and when Mother is out of earshot, I release an extended groan. I'm out of patience.

"A race between a snail and a tortoise would go faster than this battle! I shall go as mad as King George wondering what's happening out there!"

Finally I hear the fifers play a tune. Although it's familiar, I can't quite place it.

Mother announces, "Well, there it is, ladies. They've just ordered a ceasefire. And now they're playing 'parley' for surrender." She shakes her head. "So it's over then. God help us all."

I suspect there's a stubborn seed of hope planted in her mind once again. Perhaps the worst is all over, and the boorish Arnold will have the decency to leave us be.

After darkness falls like a blanket, we hear a sea of angry voices ringing out from the wharf less than a mile away. Mother and I exchange looks of disgusted resignation. Although well aware of the horrific destruction about to transpire, we are as powerless as a turtle turned on its back.

My chest grows tight as hundreds of tiny blazing torches light up the night sky in the distance. A multitude of small fires take hold, illuminating the warehouses packed with hundreds of hogsheads of tobacco. Inevitably the orange flames work their way to the rooftops where they perform a ferocious celebratory dance. Before long, the jagged blaze grows into a sprawling inferno, spreading faster than my eyes can follow.

Standing on the portico, Mother and I gape at the horrific sight unfolding in front of us. Despite breathing through a handful of rags, we are overwhelmed by coughing fits as dense smoke permeates the air. A massive wall of brilliant flames shoots up into the sky, engulfing our prized Bollings' Wharf. The warehouses groan and sag until collapsing while the fire roars like an angry dragon. The breeze blows hot ash, stinging my skin like a colony of yellow jackets. Nonetheless, we still can't bring ourselves to turn away.

Despite watching this all unfold, I still can't fathom it. Poof! Our precious warehouses are ablaze, lighting up the nighttime sky.

Mother's voice, hoarse from the heavy smoke billowing around us, is also laced with bitterness. "This is what bothers me most of all." She gestures toward the flames. "Their despicable act of cowardice created such a gorgeous feast for the eyes. I hope Arnold roasts on a bonfire in hell with Satan himself." She bends over, succumbing to another severe bout of coughing.

When she finally recovers, her voice is devoid of emotion. "Alas, he's managed to destroy our bountiful harvest after all. With a vicious wave of those torches, we've lost everything. Every last bit." She sighs with the weariness of a wounded soul. "Well, they've done it now, so we may as well go about our business. Thanks to the mercy of God, this horrific day shall soon come to an end."

As she turns to go inside, the flames illuminate her face, wet and shiny with tears. Of course she refuses to acknowledge them, let alone wipe them away. Arnold has already taken so much from her; she won't give him that, too. Once inside, she retreats to her room, but her barking cough echoes throughout the house, which is otherwise cast under a gloomy cloud of silence.

Her hacking persists much like the smoke lodged deep within my nostrils. I wash up numerous times to no avail. Eventually I'm desperate enough to plunge my entire face deep into the washbasin, way above my scalp. Despite my best efforts, though, the acrid stench persists, blocking the heavenly fragrance of the azaleas blooming outside my window. I'm destined not to sleep a wink, fearing that every creak is that devil incarnate, Arnold, approaching Bolling-brook during the dead of night.

CHAPTER 11
A MISSING SERVANT

Someone gently raps on the door in the wee hours of the morning, setting my heart pounding out of my chest. It is only a matter of seconds before Mother answers it, while I peer down the darkened stairs. Apparently she couldn't sleep either.

When Big Hank's hulking frame fills the doorway, a sense of calmness flows through my body. Thank God it's him and not the loathsome British. In the glow of the lantern, his eyes are bloodshot.

"Ma'am, don't mean to give you a fright, but want to let you know we's back. All the supplies are over at Battersea now."

"Thank you, Big Hank, for a job well done. Now you go on to sleep. Rest assured, there'll be no work come morning."

Big Hank grins broadly. "Yes, ma'am." He shifts his weight, and I'm horrified to see the fire still burning in the distance behind him. Even so, having him nearby reassures me as I go back to bed. After a while, I manage to drift off into a fitful sleep.

Hours later, I awake with a start to more knocking on the

door. I gasp, seeing my bedroom already awash in sunlight. It must be mid-morning already.

Once again, I find myself squinting down the stairs.

Whisking the door open, Mother calls out, "It's Mister Jones!" Beaming, she declares, "I was hoping to find it was you."

With bags under his eyes and his clothes filthy, Mister Jones appears exhausted but maintains his jovial nature.

"Indeed it is. Who else would be daft enough to play messenger when the battle has barely concluded?" He grins, prompting me to smile despite my anxiety. "I've but a moment to chat, but good tidings to share! I knew you'd be wondering what happened out there. I was there myself, musket in hand." He chuckles. "You know our militia is desperate for warm bodies when even a crusty old man like myself is called into service."

Mister Jones chatters on as I join Mother downstairs to drink in the news. "Our militia made quite a fine showing with musket volleys, bayonet charges, and even hand-to-hand combat. We're right proud of all our lads! Even outnumbered two-and-a-half to one, we still held them off for three hours, hiding behind buildings and fences. When we ran out of ammunition, we retreated across the Pocahontas Bridge according to plan. And the last of us took up the planks behind them while under heavy cannon fire!"

"Hip, hip, huzzah!" A beaming Mother pumps a clenched fist in the air. "Do not underestimate the bravery of our fine Virginians!"

"It's a shame General Lafayette was so far away, but at least we've given him time to set up defenses in Richmond, if the Brits continue up the James. But for now, though, we still remain in the hands of our invaders." Mister Jones sighs. "We must pray they can't find our munitions in the new location, and that they will soon be on their way."

Against the odds, though, good news awaits us later that day. Thanks to the tip from the mysterious Negro down at the wharf, the Redcoats were unable to find our military supplies. As a result, they are now departing like a fleeting tropical storm, slipping back down the James just as surreptitiously as they arrived. However, in their wake they leave a horrifying trail of destruction, including the smoking carcasses of the Virginia Navy's few ships. Glowing embers of the vast tobacco harvest still smolder from the ash-filled streets around the wharf. Hazy smoke rises from the charred remains, forming swirling pewter clouds. The pungent stench of burned tobacco hangs like a physical presence. It smells as if someone lit a thousand cigars and then tossed them aside.

I've never had a hangover before, but I imagine it would feel like this. I'm dazed and lethargic, and my brain is utterly muddled. Mother can't seem to function either. We've suffered a death: the cold-blooded murder of our livelihood. Although it didn't come as a surprise, it was still a shock to our senses.

Unfortunately work resumes the next day, and Mother ensures there's no limit to the morning chores. I suspect she wants to prevent us from dwelling on the futility of our gargantuan loss, especially herself. It's such rubbish. I'm queasy with loathing for Arnold, his mysterious guide, and the detestable King's men who brought such ruin upon us.

In addition, I'm haunted by today's new casualty list. How strange to dread something with every fiber of my being, yet tingle with impatience for it to happen. Oh, what an utter contradiction I am! Indeed the trading station is the last place in the world where I want to be, and yet the only place. In a bizarre sort of way, I'm almost happy for an excuse to escape the heavy sense of doom hanging over Bollingbrook for a few hours. Then again, I'd prefer to suffer the hell of the bloody flux or the repulsive tingling sensation of leeches on my bare skin. Alas, neither is an option. However, if there's a new list, I want to see it. I have to see it. I need to see it. It's the ultimate conundrum. I'm exhausted by my own conflicting emotions. Soon we'll know whether Stith and Alexander are dead. If only there was such thing as a "confirmed alive" list! Only that surety could put my mind at ease.

After a nerve-wracking morning of monotonous tasks and macabre thoughts, it's nearly time to go. With my work finally completed to Mother's satisfaction, I pace in front of the stables while Penny readies the carriage inside.

I'm surprised when Big Hank finds me there, his face lined with worry. He shuffles his feet and keeps his eyes cast downward. For the first time ever, he can't bring himself to look at me.

"Miss Susanna, we ain't finding Leroy nowhere. I plenty worried."

Penny comes out of the stable empty-handed, her face full of concern. "But ain't he been with you all at the courthouse?"

"No." Big Hank shakes his head and gives her a confused look. "When I was rounding up the menfolk here, I didn't see him nowhere, so we left him behind to help you all out here."

Penny stands there, slack-jawed and speechless, so I take over. "We actually haven't seen him since leaving the bee." With a stab of guilt, I recall Mother and me both rebuffing his passionate warnings several times over.

I feel a chill come over me despite the morning heat. Leroy is gone! Worse yet, from the look of things, he left two nights ago. Of course, no one knows where, not officially, but there's no need to speculate. I so want to hate him for leaving us, deserting Bollingbrook, and joining the enemy. Secretly, though, I can't find it in my heart to blame him, not after the way we treated him. Despite the suspicious disappearance of Mother's jewelry, he still didn't deserve that.

Glassy-eyed, Penny struggles to process the news. Tears

spill over and dribble down her cheeks. Finally she speaks in a raspy whisper.

"Now I ain't never gonna see my brother again."

I'm at a loss for words. What can I possibly say to comfort her right now?

Poor Penny is near collapse. "He could already be dead by now, and I don't even know it. How would I ever find out? Who going to come tell me? Nobody coming here!"

By this point I'm nauseous enough to vomit. "I'm so sorry, Penny. It's just awful how this all happened. I know you're really worried about him, and you should be. As hateful a thing he's done, he's your brother. Lord knows, I can understand that."

Without warning, Penny's jaw tightens, and her eyes grow steely. "He didn't tell me nothing, but now everyone's going to be real suspicious of me. They all going to think I'm running off too. It just ain't fair. I'd sooner fall into that well out there and drown."

Mother enters the stable for our prayer before the new casualty list. I'm afraid to tell her about Leroy's disappearance. Surely she'll fly into a rage. But I force myself, and her reaction surprises me. Her face falls, and she rests her forehead on her hand.

"Oh, no! That poor boy will not survive a week with the likes of them."

Oh, this terrible war! It leaves no one unscathed, not even the slaves. Somehow it manages to wound every single person, physically or emotionally, often both. Now it's Penny's turn, and perhaps my time of loss will take place later this morning. I can scarcely breathe.

CHAPTER 12
AN UNEXPECTED INQUISITION

We race into the trading post a few minutes after eleven. Much to my relief, the posting is late. As usual, a sizable crowd has gathered. This time, though, they're not standing there as a silent throng. They're shouting their tales of woe from the raid to anyone who will listen. Out of habit, I scan the room for Mistress Blandford, but she has no need to be here anymore. Both of her sons are dead.

The painful minutes tick by, but the ever-punctual Mister Jones fails to appear. When he finally emerges a quarter-hour later, our nerves are even more on edge than usual. Rather than hanging the list and scuttling back behind the counter, he steps forward with his hands stuffed deep into his pockets.

"For some reason unbeknown to the Inspector General or myself, we haven't received the casualty list. I feel wretched for bringing you all here in vain." He scratches his head. "I honestly don't know if there's just been a delay or if there are no further casualties to report." He flashes a nervous smile. "Of course, we all must fervently pray the latter is true."

There is a pregnant silence, heavy with palpable tension

mixed with confusion, fear, and ultimately, relief. Soon
raucous cheering, clapping, and whistling overpower the
room. I give in to hope, too, and my heart soars. Huzzah,
there is no list, not today! Perhaps his intuition is right, and
this means the last of the Guilford Courthouse casualties! Ah,
what a relief that would be, an end to worry needling me like
an angry bee trapped in my bonnet.

Mister Jones waves his hands, motioning for quiet. "However, it is still good we've all gathered here. The town crier is
standing by with a public announcement." He cups a hand
around his mouth as if sharing a secret. "It appears our illus-
trious Governor finds himself in a bit of hot water." He
signals the portly bellman forward and calls out to the crowd.
"And for the readers among you, we have the latest *Virginia
Gazette* up front."

The town crier walks with purpose into the room, and
everyone crowds around him. "Oyez, oyez! The General
Assembly of Virginia has introduced a resolution, hereby
launching an official inquisition into the Executive of our fine
Commonwealth. Governor Jefferson has been charged with
failure to provide adequate defense of Richmond when the
British invasion was imminent. They shall also determine
whether he acted with cowardice and pusillanimous conduct
in fleeing the capital during a crisis. I will post the resolution
outside immediately. There is no further information
available."

As he marches out, I let out a gasp along with so many
others. What a travesty! Our poor Governor has been
besieged by a firestorm of unforeseen trials. Political ploys
like this stinging attack will only breed more dissension. With
times so perilous, we need to maintain a united front.

"Here, here!" crow several old men. Already the huge
room is abuzz with a cacophony of voices, abandoning tradi-

tional social niceties. Much to my delight, I find myself at the center for once.

An older man bawls out in a deep voice, "Lordy, let it finally be known to all the world that Governor Jefferson disgraced us. Arnold caught him in the privy with his breeches down last January! He refused to call up the Virginia militia, even ignoring warnings from General Washington."

"Aye, he was caught unawares, but he believed the reports were false." With a start I identify the voice as mine, and my neck grows warm. I am addressing the group! Emboldened, I raise my voice a pitch and rally on. "You know full well most of them are! As Governor, he doesn't have the power to call men into military service. He can't even require them to report for duty!"

The old man admonishes me, much to my humiliation. "Now, now, missy, don't trouble yourself with such complicated matters. Haven't we discussed this before?"

In a flash I recognize him. It's Mr. Billingham, who chided me after the previous posting.

He continues his tongue-lashing. "Even your precious Jefferson would agree. After all, he said that 'Our good ladies should not wrinkle their foreheads with politics.'"

I stifle a stinging retort and keep my mouth shut. Instead I toss my head, and my eyes smart with tears. I can do far more than clean a house and have babies, but no one will give me the chance.

Voices bubble up, and the entire crowd plunges into a spirited debate. "That no-good bum deserves it! He wrote the Declaration of Independence, but he sure turned tail when the Redcoats showed up."

"But he circled Richmond for hours in the snow and rain and even needed a second horse."

"He was so afraid of them Redcoats catching him! That darn blockhead ran from the city, scared as a rabbit hiding in a foxhole. And he nailed his horse's shoes backward to look like he was headed in the opposite direction. If that ain't a coward, I don't know what is! Now why didn't that high and mighty Jefferson stay and fight like a man?"

Despite my scolding, I can't keep mum any longer. "But he did show courage! Arnold demanded all of Richmond's tobacco or he'd burn the city, and Jefferson outright refused him!"

"Listen here, little lady, that's right easy for him, living out there in Charlottesville. He ain't lost a thing in that fire! Let's send him back to his stack of books in Monticello once and for all, I tell you!"

From the back, a powerful voice with an unusual accent fills the room. "Leave the girl alone! She speaks the truth; let's stand by our Governor. Have you considered the sheer genius of the Declaration of Independence? He's hardly a coward, a dimwit, or a lazy man!"

I crane my neck to identify the speaker. My heart races at the sight of the massive swarthy-skinned Peter Francisco. Even on crutches, he is an impressive sight. A hodgepodge of bandages runs from his left knee to the top of his thigh. Feeling giddy, I can't help smirking. Betsy will be so miffed that she missed this outing!

A stooped bald man bellows out in a voice hoarse from too much tobacco, "Listen to our Virginia Giant, will you? I've heard enough hogwash to give me indigestion for a fortnight! Those Redcoats brought along handcuffs for Jefferson. Handcuffs, I tell you! So you'd have them cuff the man who wrote the Declaration like a common criminal, would you? And if he just let them take him away without trying to escape, would that show courage or just plain stupidity?"

A short man counters him. "That's tommyrot! It would never come to that!"

The bald man croaks back at the short one, "Rubbish!

They took his slaves, making quite a parade of marching them right through town. Oh, what a spectacle they'd make dragging him down to the wharf and throwing him in the bilge! And then after some pomp and circumstance, they'd sail for London and hang him at the Tower for treason! Morale here in Virginia is already at an all-time low. So how would that go over, the Lobsters lynching the man who penned the Declaration?"

Before the debate escalates into full-on fisticuffs, I slip through the crowd, find Penny in back, and shout, "Finally, no bad news!" The dull look in her eyes stops me short, so I change the subject. "That inquisition into Governor Jefferson sure makes my blood boil. He did all he possibly could during that raid, especially with his limited powers."

Then I have an epiphany that scares me to my core. Surely Arnold will get wind of this uproar and find out that Governor Jefferson is now under official investigation. Knowing Virginia is in such turmoil, he's even more likely to launch yet *another* raid. We aren't safe here, and we won't be until this horrendous war finally ends. Arnold will be back! After all, why wouldn't he?

CHAPTER 13
THE EARTH SHAKES

The next morning, Big Hank appears on the portico, his eyes only slightly less bloodshot than the day before. "Miss Sukey, I got some sad news. I was up last night helping one of the ewes birthing some lambs. All three done passed away just a bit ago." He hangs his head as if it's his fault. "They tiny legs got mixed up together."

Coming up behind me, Mother says, "Oh, what a shame. Well, thank you for your efforts, Big Hank." She turns to me. "Looks like we'll be making some candles today. Let's not let all that tallow go to naught." Her face brightens at the prospect. "Just as well. It's a perfect day to get back to the basics. Auntie Ruth has left some milk out to settle so we can churn some butter, too."

I turn my head so Mother can't see me roll my eyes. Making candles is the chore I despise most of all. It's sheer drudgery from start to finish. We melt down the foul-smelling animal fat, dip in a cotton wick, hang it on long wooden dowels, and wait for it to dry. Then we do this painstaking task over and over again, just for one batch! I detest it enough in the fall after we've slaughtered livestock for winter meat. Oh, what an ungodly stink! I can't even imagine the stench in the infernal heat of the summer kitchen today. I can't think of anything more horrendous!

Although I'm willing to do anything to avoid the misery of candle duty, I don't dare voice my complaints for fear of getting my ears boxed.

"Mother, Penny and I will churn the butter for Auntie Ruth." When she gives an absent-minded nod, I'm elated. Although churning is also tedious scut work, at least it doesn't involve such repulsive odors. "And we'll bring the churns out to the barn to make more room in the kitchen." I head off with Penny in tow before Mother has a chance to object.

By the time we have lugged the wooden churns out to the barn, sweat has already soaked through my long-sleeved shift and moistened my apron. Nevertheless we set about the duty at hand, plunging our dashers up and down. Within minutes, my arms are already aching.

"Oh, how I hate this dreadful task! I'm already exhausted, and we've barely begun."

A stern voice barks out of nowhere. "Stop your grumbling, Sukey! It's far better to be bored than terrified!" Startled, the dasher falls from my hands. Swiveling my head, I'm horrified to see Mother outlined in the barn door way, her back ramrod straight and hands perched on her hips. I want to dart into an empty horse stall, latch the door, and hide. But I'm frozen in place; I couldn't move if I tried.

Mother's eyes narrow as she walks toward me, wagging her finger. "You should be grateful you're out of harm's way unlike so many other unfortunates. They'd give anything to be here, their bellies full, and safe within the walls Father built for us."

I can't meet her eyes; I'm too ashamed. "Yes, ma'am."

"Let's count our many blessings, shall we?" Mother waves

her hands, gesturing to our opulent surroundings. "You never know when Fate, and especially King George, might conspire to take them all away."

Then in a flash, she's gone just as quickly as she arrived. Penny and I get back to work, plunging in a steady rhythm as the churns shake and issue a whooshing sound. Impressed, I declare, "It's amazing these churns put off such strong vibrations!" As I pause to wipe my brow before beads of sweat roll into my eyes, the dirt floor moves ever so slightly.

"Penny, stop for a minute! Why is the ground shaking?" We freeze and look around the barn with suspicious eyes as if expecting Satan himself to jump out of the shadows.

Dumbfounded, we stare at each other, now noticing a low rumbling sound. She mumbles, "It sound like an army marching."

As we run to the doorway, I shout, "No! It can't be!" Over the crest of our hill, a line of Redcoats extends off into the distance like tiny red ants crawling along in formation. Shrieking at the top of my lungs, I sprint into the sweltering summer kitchen, oblivious for once to the revolting smell of melting sheep fat.

Mother scowls at me. "Sukey, how unbecoming! What in the world has gotten into you?"

Suddenly out of breath, I gasp, "The British are coming!" She stares at me, her mouth agape. I gesture outside. "Come, see for yourself! They're out there marching!" We dart outside followed by the slaves and stare into the horizon.

Putting a hand to her chest, Mother breathes, "Good God, you're right! That blasted Arnold is back! Let's pray to God he passes us by, but we must prepare for the worst. Come, get inside!"

I shiver despite the sweat coating my body. Taking in shallow breaths, my lungs push back against the confines of my tightly laced stays. Desperate, I shake my head, hoping to make this horrible scene vanish.

Barking over her shoulder, Mother charges toward the house with Harriet just inches behind, sucking in air in loud gulps. "Sukey and Penny, come quickly!" Penny and I remain transfixed, though, gaping at the horror unfolding off in the distance. When we don't move, she circles back, her gown billowing around her.

Gathering me in close, Mother speaks in a low, calm voice. "I don't know why in God's name that despicable Arnold is back. Hopefully they'll pass us by. But if those vermin do come here, stay back and do whatever they say. I wish to God your father and brothers were here, but we'll handle it, you and I." She gives me a grim smile, her thin lips pursed. "They'll surely know we're Patriots here, so don't meddle with them. Leave it to me. Come now, both of you! I need your help."

Try as I might, I can't utter a sound. After nudging Penny and me into the house, Mother races into the parlor, with Harriet still hot on her heels. As if in a trance, we trail along behind her. Mother claps her hands. "Come now, let's gather up all the valuables! That vile turncoat will surely scoop up everything, just like in Philadelphia, and Lord knows, there certainly won't be a court-martial for him this time."

Mother whirls around to Harriet. "Head out to the portico and keep a lookout! Let us know if they head this way!"

Harriet nods as tears run down her face. "Yes, ma'am. I'm ready to do my part, yes, ma'am. Lordy, them soldiers out there scare me like the devil himself. None of us Negroes want them taking us nowhere. No, ma'am. We heard too many stories, that's right." Every few words, she puffs in and out as if in the throes of childbirth.

"Sukey, come over here with me! Penny, take down the

portraits and pile them on the dining table. I shan't give that Arnold the satisfaction of torching ours like they did at the Harrisons! And take extra care with Mister Bolling's over the mantle!"

I want to weep; I've studied Father's portrait for years, memorizing his every line and curve. I love that we share our oval faces, almond-shaped hazel eyes, and auburn hair. I can't bear the thought of its destruction.

"Wrap them up in the fine linens and bring them down to the tunnel! They can have the rest for all I care." She tosses her head. "Fast! Go!" She claps her hands again, but Penny's already in motion, back to her steadfast self once again.

Grabbing a large basket, Mother bustles about gathering up our prized heirlooms. Immobilized, I feel like an observer from afar. Detached, I watch Mother grab fistfuls of sterling silverware and stuff it in various teapots and vases, making a cacophony of clinking sounds. Lastly she shoves a smattering of pewter candlesticks willy-nilly into the empty crevices; the scant remains of her once vast collection.

With a resounding thud, she slams the stuffed vessels down onto her remaining silver tray. "At least there's far less to hide since so much is already gone. If it wasn't for our woodworkers and silver utensils, we'd eat with our hands." Earlier in the war, once ammunition became scarce, Mother gave away every item made of lead. Then when lead became scarce, she sacrificed her pewter mugs, melting them down into bullets herself. "But it was well worth the sacrifice! I'm proud of the many musket balls we provided. I only wish to lodge one in Benedict Arnold's heart, if he still has one!" Mother cackles as if impressed by her own spite.

After plunking two urns and a tea set down onto the platter, she thrusts it at me. Still in shock, I hold my arms out like a wooden doll. Within seconds, Mother grabs another tray and sets about filling it. "Father built this house himself, and the King's men aren't going to destroy it if I've anything to say about it! Now come along, Sukey, down to the cellar! We'll see this through. You just watch! Mind the stairs now, lest you go arse over teakettle."

I gaze at Mother's retreating back. With a lump in my throat, I can't manage any response. Crouching down to keep myself steady, I shuffle down the steep wooden steps behind her. Thankfully, the cellar's earthy coolness calms my jangled nerves. Despite its recent airing-out, a familiar musty odor still permeates the area.

Mother plunks her overflowing basket on the dirt floor and grabs a lantern. "Put it anywhere you can find a spot. I'll open the tunnel while you and Penny gather more." After several attempts at lighting it, the lantern finally casts a dim glow. She opens the door along the far wall, revealing a cavern of blackness. Clouds of dust waft through the air followed by a blanket of damp chilliness, a foreboding of the sinister force invading City Point.

Holding the lantern aloft, Mother scuttles into the brick-lined tunnel, her low heels clicking. "Keep bringing everything down as fast as your feet can carry you! Go! Empty to the hutch, and remember to wrap the china in the tablecloths!"

Tucking my chin, I race up the narrow stairs and slam into Penny who has the portraits piled to her chin. With bulging eyes, she staggers backward as her precious pile teeters. Terrified of damaging Father's beloved portrait, I reach out to steady her. After a nerve-wracking moment, her precarious stack settles back in line. We exchange sighs of relief, especially thankful that Mother didn't witness our near disaster. Then up and down we go like a seesaw, hiding my family's treasured belongings.

With almost superhuman strength, Mother hauls the cargo into the tunnel while jabbering away in a frenzied state.

"This was always Father's favorite place. He said it lets you escape from the world." Wiping her hands on her apron, she frowns. "I've got quite a mind to disappear right now, but I won't give that traitorous fool any such satisfaction. If he dares to come here and set fire to this house, he shall do it while my eyes bore into his skull! And if he has the gall to quarter here, one thing is for sure." She raises an index finger in the semi-darkness. "With God as my witness, I shan't restrain myself from strangling him in the darkness of the night!" She releases a maniacal cackle. "How I would relish such a task!"

Racing upstairs for another load, I shudder. Of course such a bold act would make Mother a celebrated Patriot heroine, but the price is much too high. They'd surely hang her, perhaps me too, and confiscate every slave. The Redcoats would make quite a sport of transforming dear Bollingbrook into a pile of charred rubble that would smoke for days on end. Hopefully Mother values our plantation and everyone who depends on it more than such revenge, albeit well deserved.

Harriet lets out a blood-curling scream that echoes through the floorboards. Then, almost hyperventilating, she shrieks her message between forced breaths. "Mistis! You best come up here right quick! The British! They be coming right here to Bollingbrook!"

Shedding her ladylike persona, Mother yells at the top of her lungs, "Bugger! I thought we were done with our part! Will this godforsaken war never end before it ruins every last one of us?" Her raw emotion shakes me to the core. She never despairs, not ever. It isn't in her constitution, not until now.

Harriet hollers down the stairs again, "Great God almighty, Mistis! Look at them all out there! Sure enough, they be coming here, straight away to Bollingbrook! I ain't never seen the likes of this, no ma'am! Lord, have mercy!"

Despite the distance, her heavy moans fill the dank air, mournful like a dying cow.

Enraged, Mother shouts back, "I've never seen the likes of this either! Only in my worst nightmares! Yell when you see the whites of their eyes!"

Harriet breaks out in wracking sobs. "I been out there bringing in water all day long. I ain't seen nothing coming up river. Not one gunboat, no ma'am!"

"What does that insufferable Arnold want with us again?" Mother stamps her foot. "We certainly haven't any tobacco left if that's what he's after! Doesn't that loathsome turncoat remember burning our warehouses? And all of Richmond's back in January? I suppose he wants a second chance at finding our munitions supply. But why, pray tell, is he headed to Bolingbrook of all places? Does he think it's hidden here?"

With loathing in my heart, I feel dread wash over me like a tidal wave. The answer is obvious as much as she doesn't want to acknowledge it. He's decided to quarter here, and we've heard too many horrifying stories about this abomination to count. King George's appalling Quartering Act empowers these cruel and vengeful British soldiers to overrun our homes at will. They always arrive like this, an immense invasive force without warning, now looking more like an onslaught of giant red cicadas than soldiers. In reality, though, they're far worse, akin to maggots already feasting on an animal that has yet to die. While on the premises, they have the right to eat, drink, and loot everything. Naturally there isn't a thing we can do about it. Worse yet, they often burn the plantation in their wake, confiscating the slaves and horses as they depart.

Hoping to distract her, I gesture to wooden casks and hogsheads filled with ale, cider, rum, whiskey, and brandy. Wine bottles are stacked on top and next to the canned preserves and dried fruit piled up on the floor. "What about all this drink? Shall we hide it too? If we don't, they'll just guzzle it all!"

"Let's give them all they can drink. They can partake until they're boozy for all I care, provided they don't lay a hand on us. After all, our goal is to survive this invasion with Bolling-brook intact." Her voice cracks with bitterness while I breathe a silent sigh of relief. At least, she isn't serious about strangling Arnold after all, however tempting a proposition. "Should we be so lucky, perhaps they'll drown themselves in too much ale. That's the only thing preventing me from poisoning the whole lot of them!" She slams a box of silver onto the brick floor, startling me with the din, and setting off clouds of dust.

"Come now, Sukey, start handing it all over to me," she calls, her voice tight and controlled. A wave of nervous energy washes over me. I pass the stacks of china and stuffed baskets to her while coughing into my sleeve.

Much to my horror, I hear the familiar clippety-clop of horses making their way to Bollingbrook. Within seconds, though, it becomes a ferocious pounding, as a multitude of hooves thunder down our lane. It grows even louder, almost deafening. The vibrations are so strong I feel like I'm on horseback myself.

When Penny and I scurry upstairs for yet another haul of heirlooms, we can't help but stop and stare out the window, mesmerized. It's impossible to process. A horrendous influx of enemy troops is advancing toward us, a bona fide night-mare in living form. I clap a hand over my mouth as prickles run like needles from my neck to the small of my back. Our country lane is now teeming with Redcoats creeping like giant red ants with Brown Bess muskets for stingers. There's no mistaking it. This terrifying parade of soldiers is heading toward Bollingbrook at full speed. Lo and behold, the British cavalry leads the way, clad in their notorious green. Of course,

Stith immediately comes to mind. How I wish he were here with me, Alexander too, now more than ever.

Gaping at the fearsome sight, tears well up in Penny's round eyes which spill over, trickling down her ashen face. I can't begin to comfort her as I'm on the verge of full-fledged panic myself. My insides churn like the butter we've been making as I wring my hands on my apron. All I can do is stare, mesmerized by the abomination unfolding right in front of me.

The presiding officer rides several strides in front of this imposing procession, upright and regal in his saddle, staring dead ahead. The dreaded Arnold is back; it can't be anyone else but him. After all, he's the Commander of the British Army in Virginia. His deputy trots along several lengths behind him, his chest and a thigh both heavily bandaged. Drummers come around the bend, beating the steady British march, much slower than the breakneck pace of my heart. Then the Regulars traipse in, row after row in a never-ending stream stirring up massive gray clouds of dust into which I'd love to disappear.

As the first columns draw closer, a number of soldiers appear wounded, many seriously so. The questions running through my head multiply. Aren't these dreaded Redcoats coming from Arnold's headquarters in Portsmouth just down-river? So how did they come to be in such a wretched state? And where did they land their ships?

Mother calls for us, so Penny and I find it within ourselves to bring down another load.

It's hard to believe that an hour ago making butter felt like such a burden. As usual, Mother was correct. It's far better to be bored than terrified.

CHAPTER 14
A RED SEA OF LOBSTERS

H arriet calls down in a thin, shaky voice. "Mistis, they be coming! I see the whites of their eyes. Yes, ma'am! Soon they be marching up the steps." She scuttles down the first few steps and peers into the darkness, her bulging eyes illuminated like miniature moons. "Lawd, have mercy! Mistis, please don't be making me stay up there all by myself to face them Lobsters. If they get any closer, I be wetting myself sure enough."

Eventually the lead horses neigh and bristle as they come to a stop. Heavy boots thud up the front steps onto the portico. Within seconds a fist pounds on the door, several times in quick succession and forceful enough to come right through it. Then a deep voice booms with even more authority than the town crier.

"British Army at the ready. Under the Quartering Act of His Majesty King George III, open up immediately! I hereby announce the arrival of Lieutenant General Lord Charles Cornwallis, Commander of the British Southern Forces, and his Deputy Commander, Brigadier General Charles O'Hara."

Tugging on a heavy tray laden with china, I let go with a

gasp. Losing my footing, I topple over backward, hitting the dirt floor with a profound thump. With my skirt above my knees, I lie there in a daze. So it isn't that vile Arnold after all! I've been preparing myself for his big nose and legendary glowing gray eyes. Even worse, though, it's Cornwallis himself! But that's impossible, isn't it? Normally it would take a week or more to move such a massive army. There's no way the British Southern Army could've traveled all that distance without any Patriots detecting them en route. Or did they manage to do just that?

Mother curses as her face drains to an alabaster white. "Mother of God, it's not Arnold! It's god-awful Cornwallis himself, with his entire army creeping along behind him! I don't know which one I detest more!" Grabbing her hem, she emerges from the tunnel, her eyes blazing and lips pursed in a grim line.

While Arnold is vicious and detested beyond measure, Cornwallis is notorious for leaving utter devastation in his wake. He razes homesteads for sport and absconds with anything and everything of value, especially Negroes, horses, and food in any form. Once Cornwallis leaves his mark on a Patriot's homestead, it's never the same place again. More often than not, it no longer exists.

Dumfounded, I yank down my gown. "So they've given up on North Carolina, just like that?" The small of my back throbs, but the adrenaline rushing through my body masks the pain. Cornwallis, the Commander of the British Southern Army, is on our very doorstep! But how can this be? He would never withdraw from North Carolina after sacrificing so much trying to conquer it. Or would he? Perhaps Commanding General Clinton ordered him to abandon it altogether. Then after the enormous casualties at Guilford Courthouse, he was too low on troops to leave behind an occupying force. However, by moving on, he forfeits the land he fought so hard to conquer. My bewildered mind circles back to the same question. Why? I can't fathom his motivation. Why would he abandon such a colossal investment of time, sweat, and blood just to hightail it here to the sleepy Old Dominion?

"Dear God in heaven, we shall soon find out whether we want to or not," Mother murmurs, wiping her hands on her soiled cotton apron and tossing it onto the dirt floor. "I am off to meet this filth face to face, but I shan't curtsy to him. I'd rather that he tar and feather me himself!" She adjusts her yellowed mobcap, takes a deep breath, and trots up the stairs, her back straight and head held high.

Harriet plods along behind her as if heavy chains bind her ankles. Between bouts of deep breathing, she chants under her breath. "Lawd, have mercy."

Mother calls back over her shoulder. "Sukey, once you're finished, move the hutch in front of the door. If all goes to naught, the tunnel could end up being our only hiding place." Her voice takes on a bitter edge. "If you need them, there are axes and shovels in there."

From the top of the stairs, she peers back down at me. In a low, hushed voice she commands, "Stay down there! I'll fetch you myself once all is safe. If they see you coming up, they'll know exactly where to find our valuables." Mother's voice softens, and her eyes mist in the haze of the lantern. "Remember, Sukey, you're more precious to me than anything in this house."

Even in my worst nightmares, I've never contemplated the enemy occupying our home. As Penny and I hide the portraits and heirlooms, I can't hold back my hot tears a minute longer. I swipe at my flushed cheeks with the back of my hand, flooded with admiration for Mother while I cower down here in relative safety. Perhaps it's time to accept the unpleasant truth. I'm a helpless simpleton of a girl, and chicken-hearted as well. If only I could face danger without freezing like a birdbath during a cold snap.

An aristocratic voice booms through the floorboards, loud enough to echo off the cellar walls. "Good day, Madam. I am Lieutenant General Lord Charles Cornwallis, Commander of the Southern Forces, here in His Majesty's service. Have I the pleasure of speaking with the mistress of this plantation?"

Penny and I exchange looks of consternation. This is Cornwallis himself speaking! Heavens, his cultured voice oozes with the refinement of high nobility. I hold my breath, bracing myself for Mother's reply.

"Good afternoon, General." I swear Mother's voice quavers, but I don't trust my ears. "Indeed, I am Mistress Susanna Bolling of Bollingbrook Plantation."

He continues on, his voice clipped. "Lady Bolling, please summon the gentleman of the house immediately." I can't believe what I'm hearing; Mother must be bristling. General Cornwallis is second only to General Clinton, England's Commander-in-Chief. Is he really on our doorstep, the same one I cross over countless times a day? Terrified as I am, it's a curious relief the dreaded Benedict Arnold hasn't returned. Despite Cornwallis's many atrocities, at least he isn't a traitor. Perhaps Mother will find it easier to refrain from strangling him. I certainly hope so.

Mother responds, her voice softer. "He is not present, sir."

Cornwallis interrupts her. "I see. Shall I assume he is off committing treason against our King?"

I picture Mother upstairs looking this forbidding General in the eye. "Sir, that is certainly not the case. My husband passed away a decade ago after serving in the Virginia House of Burgesses for years." Her voice is stronger now, more confident. Of course she has neglected to mention that Father pursued the same radical agenda as General Washington,

Governor Jefferson, Patrick Henry, and Richard Bland from across the river.

"My condolences, Lady Bolling. I myself lost my wife recently." After a pause, the General clears his throat and resumes a rougher tone. "As for your sons, am I correct in assuming they are rebels then?"

"No, sir, indeed not. They proudly serve in the army of their country, fighting invaders from three thousand miles away. Therefore, they are not rebels at all." My heart pounds as I wait for his reaction. Certainly Mother knows better than to antagonize Cornwallis any further! After all, British soldiers are swarming all over Bollingbrook like bees in an overcrowded hive.

"Lady Bolling, I fear we differ in opinion. A friend to his country will be a friend to our King, who is our master."

Mother doesn't hesitate for a second. "In this country only slaves acknowledge a master."

I gasp and clap a hand over my mouth. Her manner is so provocative, downright brazen even. Is she goading the General to retaliate on purpose?

The General speaks at a higher volume as if to drown out her cheekiness. Although mannerly, his voice drips with condescension. "Madam, as you suspect, my Southern Army has moved north into Virginia after our latest victory at Guilford Courthouse."

Penny and I exchange scowls at the word 'victory.'

"My scouts directed me here as the most considerable house in the village. Therefore, the service of His Majesty requires the occupation of your property. As such, I shall take up quarters here."

"As you wish. Right now my family consists of only my daughter, our Negroes, and myself. We are your captives."

Thankfully, General Cornwallis chooses to ignore her barb. "Accordingly, my men shall occupy all the available outbuildings and open areas, including the fields. As you may suspect, the remainder of my Southern Army shall quarter throughout City Point as well. General O'Hara and Lieutenant Colonel Tarleton, both wounded, shall stay in the residence with me, and we shall dine here with my Senior Staff this evening. We depart tomorrow at dawn on a vital mission. Then this inconvenience shall come to an end, and you can return to your domestic tranquility."

I imagine Cornwallis's patronizing smile and seethe at his trivialization of our life. The unexpected arrival of an entire army of enemy soldiers on our doorstep is nothing more than an "inconvenience?" And what "vital mission" is there in Virginia of all places?

Compounding my fury, Banastre Tarleton, better known as "Bloody Ban," will sleep in our house – in my brother's bed, no less! He's infamous for showing no mercy and taking no prisoners. Despised among Patriots for unparalleled savagery, he earned another nickname, "the Butcher," for massacring hundreds of Virginians at the Battle of Waxhaws down in South Carolina. Even more appalling, the soldiers were surrendering, many down on their knees.

However, I take smug satisfaction that we wounded him at Guilford Courthouse. In fact, I know he lost two fingers during the battle. It wasn't nearly enough suffering for him, but at least we avenged ourselves in part. Despite my devout Anglican upbringing, I wish him nothing but searing pain, burning in the fires of hell for all eternity.

Cornwallis continues with an irritable edge to his voice. "Lady Bolling, might we step inside and escape this blistering Virginia sun of yours?"

"Certainly, General." Mother's voice is polite but cold.

As Penny and I ferry more prized possessions into the tunnel, heavy boots stomp into the house above us like a herd of cattle. The floorboards that Father installed with such love now groan and bow under the excessive weight. My gaze floats upward, fearful Cornwallis and his henchmen will fall through the ceiling any second.

"So this is Bollingbrook on Mansion Hill? I was told it is the finest in the area." He sniffs with disdain. "The remainder of my men are quartering elsewhere along the river."

I picture his aristocratic nose pointed in the air. It's a wonder I could hear him with the ferocious pounding of my heart. Although I scoff at his pretension, my knees shake like there's an earthquake underfoot. Apparently the finest Georgian house in Prince George County just can't compete with his bonny old England!

For two days after the Battle of Guilford Courthouse, the Redcoats became separated from their camp and slept out in the pouring rain. Surely our Bollingbrook is preferable to those blood-saturated fields, reeking of hundreds of decomposing bodies. Cornwallis has no right at all to be here, let alone belittling the quarters taken by force and intimidation. He should be beyond grateful to step foot on our lovely plantation and for every morsel of nourishment stolen from its grounds.

Suddenly I realize that our neighbors are under siege as well, including Betsy. As much as I loathe her, I hope she is coping better than me.

"Indeed it is, sir." Although Mother must be choking back a stinging retort, her voice is strong and steady.

I breathe a long exhale, thankful for both.

By this point, Mother doesn't sound perturbed in the least, like facing off with an enemy general is part of an ordinary day. I picture her determined eyes daring to hold his gaze. If only I could exhibit such courage instead of trembling down in the cellar like a ninny about to faint with fright.

"Sir, I've heard loathsome tales of men looting, burning homes, and making off with slaves. We implore you to act with common decency and refrain from such destruction. In exchange, we shall offer you the finest Virginia hospitality we can muster." A defenseless widow surrounded by a massive enemy army, even she accepts that she has no leverage.

"Yes, Madam, as you wish. Contrary to what your Whig sources may have told you, we are not the barbarians who initiated this uprising." His tone drips with bitterness. "It is your rebel soldiers who insist upon their barbaric tactics." He sniffs again. "Of course, we would have put down this insurrection long ago had they conducted themselves as proper gentlemen."

General Cornwallis continues, presumably still looking down his nose at Mother. "As for General Arnold, no one, including myself, sanctions his past conduct. I'm sure you will be delighted that I have taken command of his troops and dispatched him back to New York. That being said, I must remind you that the owner of Berkeley Plantation committed the highest form of treason in signing that mutinous Declaration and leading meetings for those blasphemous Articles of Confederation. He should consider himself quite fortunate that he and his family escaped with their lives."

Dead silence follows as I exchange worried glances with Penny. We stand frozen, afraid to move. Presumably Mother is doing all she can to stifle a bitter rebuke. As the stillness persists, though, I can't help but squirm. Surely even Mother can't get away with snubbing General Cornwallis again, especially not with his entourage present. Clearing her throat, Mother finally speaks almost a whisper. "Thank you, sir."

I let out a sigh of relief. Huzzah, it's over!

But Mother's not done. "Because if that was your plan, I would destroy it all right now to prevent you the use of it." Mother has what she wants, his pledge to preserve Bollingbrook. At this point she's either deliberately antagonizing him or has lost her mind; perhaps both. Of course, we've heard the tale of the courageous Patriot woman who recently torched her own home and wheat fields in North Carolina. Perhaps General Cornwallis doesn't have the patience to deal with another strong-willed Patriot woman, despite her absence of bargaining power.

Another uncomfortable silence follows, now from General Cornwallis. After a muffled cough, he acquiesces. "So be it." Then he mutters, "Even in their dresses, the females seem to bid us in defiance."

I smile in the darkness. Leave it to Mother's tart tongue to put General Cornwallis in his place! I can only hope and pray he'll be true to his word. Unfortunately we won't know until his loathsome army finally removes its tentacles from our home.

Oh my, she now has the gall to add another demand. "Sir, with all due respect, my daughter is also here in the residence. I request your assurance she will remain unbothered by your men."

"Certainly, Madam. As you said, provided we are treated to the best of your hospitality, we shall endeavor to do the same. These men have survived a fearsome battle, suffered the bloody pox, and then marched in this horrid Southern heat with little rest and scant provisions. Rest assured, they are far too exhausted and weakened by heatstroke to disturb your young lady. However, I can assure you anyone caught ogling will face the harshest of discipline. Suffice it to say, I've already made an example of two ruffians for such conduct during our march here."

Feeling like a little girl hiding behind Mother's skirt, I flush. Mother could wrangle my nerves without effort, but no doubt she'll protect me above all else. I want to race up the narrow stairs and stand by her side so we can face our malicious invaders together. There are certainly limits to what one human being can shoulder alone, even someone as fearless as Mother.

Emboldened, I am creeping up a step and then another when I feel a tug on my hem. I fish an arm behind myself to free it. Now there's a slight pinch to the back of my arm. I turn to see Penny waving her hands in the semi-darkness. She mouths and half-whispers, "Miss Sukey, you best stay here like Mistress said. She doing just fine up there."

I blink. Surely this is the closest Penny has ever come to issuing me an order. I back down the steps. She's right after all, as her sensibilities usually are. Now that General Cornwallis has assured my safety, we must protect the Bolling valuables. Besides, Mother is doing just dandy up there, despite her quarrelsome comments.

"As I said, my men are faint from hunger, dehydration, and fatigue after our recent victory." Cornwallis's voice has an edge of irritability. "We have marched from sun up to sun down for days on end in this infernal heat. We ask that you prepare victuals and drink in the greatest quantities available."

Oh, the nerve of it all! Anger pulsates through every fiber of my body. This enemy army just slaughtered hundreds of Patriots at Guilford Courthouse, including Joseph. Now we have to sacrifice every bit of our limited resources to nourish these murderers without a murmur of protest. Indubitably, these Lobsters will devour it all like starving wolves over a fresh kill. If these uniformed murderers haven't already killed my brothers as well, they'll still gladly ram a bayonet through their hearts given half a chance.

"We shall also fill the residence." General Cornwallis orders his adjutant to count the rooms.

"However, we shall allow you to keep your sleeping chamber, Lady Bolling, for you and your daughter."

How magnanimous to allow Mother to sleep in her own bed. As I bristle with indignation, I can only imagine her reaction! So they're taking over my room as well, sleeping in my very own bed, leaving me to cower with Mother in her four-poster. Of course, I'll feel much safer there, but the indignity of it all rankles with me, deep down in my bones. To suffer an invasion like this, it just isn't right! Frustration bubbles up within me, threatening to spill over. Alas, as usual, there's nothing I can do. There's no way a Patriot girl can fight back against a British General, especially when he has his army at the ready outside our front door.

The adjutant returns, announcing that General Cornwallis will occupy my room. Perhaps even more repulsive, though, Colonel Tarleton will spend the night next door in Stith's bed. General O'Hara will take Alexander's room. Although equally swallowed up by fear and enraged by this repulsive occupation, I can't help but take solace. Since Mother's bedroom is on the main floor, at least a flight of stairs will separate us from our vile captors.

I have a mind to climb onto the roof tonight and set the house ablaze. With that, I could eliminate Cornwallis, General O'Hara, and of course the wicked Butcher. Regaining my senses, though, I push the far-fetched plan out of my mind. Alas, such daydreams are futile; it's high time to accept reality. As Mother said, we're nothing more than prisoners in our own home. Oh, to be so powerless! There's nothing I can do to change our situation or the outcome of this grisly war. I'd only create more strife than anyone could ever imagine.

I whisper to Penny, "What are we going to do? If the other General sees us coming up the stairs, everything down here will be lost. But they'll find us down here soon enough. It won't be long before they do a full search of the house. We may as well just hand it all over on Mother's favorite silver tea tray."

Penny withdraws for a moment and then perks up. "How

about we hide in the tunnel? We can shut the door behind us."

"Still though, what do we do next? That laid-up General may never leave the house! And if there's a Regular standing guard upstairs, he'll hear us coming up those creaky steps!"

"Then we have one choice, Miss Sukey." Penny takes a deep breath. "We have to go out the other way."

I'm flabbergasted. "You mean go out to the dock? Are you mad? And face all those Redcoats head on? We'd walk right into the heart of Cornwallis's army!"

"Miss Sukey, can't you hear all that ruckus still going on out there? Sounds like more folks be marching in, so you know the rest of them are busy waiting or setting up camp. The dock should be clear for a bit yet. We'd best go now while we can." I give her a skeptical look, but she persists. "I don't like it neither, but we ain't got no choice. Soon those Regulars will be all over that dock, soaking their sweaty feet and fishing to fill their bellies. If we go right now, we be fine. The longer we wait, the worse it be getting."

I sigh. "All right, Penny, I don't have a better idea." Perhaps Penny and I can then walk to the big house as if we'd been on the river, not hiding valuables in our secret tunnel.

Leaving the door slightly ajar, we push the shelves in front. We then squeeze behind them and pull the door shut. Once in the brick-lined tunnel, I hold the lantern aloft to see our way. Nearing the exit, I notice two large water pitchers. "Let's carry these out there and fill them. Nothing unusual about that!" I shrug, forgetting I've never once had to gather water. That backbreaking job used to belong to Leroy eight-to-ten times a day, but now falls to Penny and Harriet.

As we emerge onto the dock, the bright sun comes as a shock. It's no matter since I don't dare look anywhere but down. Penny and I kneel down and whisk our pitchers through the water, filling them to the brim. The surprising weight requires that I use both hands, unlike Penny. Finally I summon the courage to sneak a few furtive glances; I can feel my eyes bug out. Regulars swarm over our plantation like a mammoth red rug blanketing the land, covering everything but the river itself. Thankfully we're behind the crowd, so no one has noticed us; not yet, anyway.

Emboldened, I survey the layer of filth enveloping them like a heavy fog as if they haven't washed in months, which they probably haven't. Sprawling black bloodstains spot their unkempt coats, now faded to pink from the glaring sun. Previously white, their breeches and leggings are now deep shades of mud and grime. Most suffer from a limp of sorts, some grievously wounded with the rest perhaps just footsore.

Needless to say, I'm shocked to find the world's most powerful army in such a sorry state. In a twisted way, though, it heartens me. At long last, the firm Patriot resolve has weakened them almost beyond recognition! However, it also serves as a cruel reminder, disturbing me to my core. Without a doubt our Continental Army is far worse off, including my brothers.

Yet more Regulars pour into Bollingbrook, swarming like a phalanx of bees toward an already overflowing hive. It's a vast sea of sallow and unshaven faces with eyes as red-rimmed and droopy as a pack of old hounds'. They mill around the outbuildings, absorbing every resource before everything is depleted. They inundate the washhouse, desperate to clean their layered wool uniforms, grimy and reeking of sweat and dried blood. With their scrawny horses drooping with exhaustion, haggard soldiers queue up at the blacksmith shop, encircling the building several times within minutes. There isn't a man or a horse without a serious need for attention.

The Regulars carry nothing but their muskets, kidney-shaped tin canteens, and the battered uniforms on their

weary backs. They have no additional gear, not even a haver-
sack, and quickly disperse. Lining the riverbank, they alter-
nate between chugging water and pouring it overhead in a
cascade while exploding in whoops and hollers. Others have
already shed their filthy clothing to float in the cool water of
the Appomattox. Their tiny heads bob up and down, dotting
the river as far as I can see.

Next comes the Herculean task that Penny and I both
dread. We must make our way through the massive influx of
Redcoats to the front steps. As we set out, I'm struck with
the noxious stench of their grimy bodies. After a cough, I
switch to breathing through my mouth. Then a rustling
sound bubbles up from within the crowd. I gasp as the Regulars shuffle back a step, almost in unison, clearing a narrow
path for us.

With the parting of this red sea of troops, the sharp gazes
of hundreds of enemy soldiers bore into my skull. Some
scrappy-looking soldiers leer at me with oily smirks. Others
wear an open look of pity, taking me by surprise. This is most
disconcerting; I didn't expect the slightest sign of compas-
sion. Although part of a gargantuan army, though, they're all
people, still individuals, I suppose. In my mind, I've always
lumped all Redcoats together as one faceless entity of vicious
oppression. Perhaps some serve for no other reason than
because their King demands it. My heart hardens. Those
soldiers are probably the exception.

With growing discomfort, I look down, comforted by the
familiar sight of my round-toed leather shoes with their
prominent brass buckles. In contrast, the soldiers' footwear is
so torn and ragged it could only offer scant protection at
best. Many don't have shoes at all, only rough strips of
cowhide tied around their feet with neck weed. It's a wonder
they marched two hundred miles with the hot sun beating
down on them every step of the way. Hopefully my brothers

are fortunate enough to have shoes, but I know how unlikely that is. War makes no exceptions for anyone, not even for a family dating back to the Jamestown. It doesn't matter if Pocahontas is your great-grandmother. If there aren't any provisions, then all soldiers go without.

"Those steps have never been so far away!" I mutter to Penny.

Penny squeezes in closer to me. "Let's just keep ourselves moving, Miss Sukey. One step at a time. We'll be just fine soon enough."

The crowd becomes even denser. A raspy-voiced Regular calls out to me in a mocking tone. "Well, well, if it isn't Miss Molly Pitcher herself. We just love your fine plantation here. Oh, Miss Molly Pitcher, might I have a swallow of your fine Virginia water? You can just pour it right down my parched gullet." I keep walking, wishing I had a free hand to clutch Penny's elbow.

As we move through the parted sea, a Regular pushes his way toward us. "What? Molly Pitcher won't even give a quick slug to a thirsty soldier?" He slaps his hand to his forehead, feigning light-headedness. "I'm about to perish for want of a mere gulp!"

I grit my teeth and strengthen my grip on the pitcher. I'm tempted to throw it in his smarmy face. Biting my lip, though, I remain steadfast, refusing to acknowledge his taunting.

He raises his voice, intensifying his mockery. "What, you can't spare even a sip of water? Just look at us poor miserable blokes so happy to see your pretty face! Oh, Molly Pitcher, we've been marching day after day; forever, it seems. Can't we get even a drop of sympathy from you?" The crowd ripples with laughter.

He throws his tricorne hat to the ground, and his tone changes to disgust. "You Virginia dames are just as blamed feisty as those Tar Heels down in Carolina." Hoots of agreement ring out. Honored by the comparison, warmth fills my chest. Perhaps I'm braver than I believe.

Suddenly burning with indignation, I can't stand for his heckling a moment longer. After all, they are the invaders! This is my home, and I am on my family's land! I have every right to act as I please without ridicule from such a brute. As anger surges through my body, I lunge forward, ready to confront my vile tormentor.

At the same time, Penny yanks my elbow, pulling me back toward her. "He don't matter one bit, Miss Sukey. That scaly loggerhead ain't fit to shine your shoes! We almost there."

As we pass the ornery soldier, he steps forward and blocks our path with his hands on his hips. His defiant smirk reveals yellowed, crooked teeth. "What's the matter, Molly Pitcher? Oh dear me, do I have it wrong?" He gives an exaggerated bow and steps forward, coming within inches of me. His foul body odor washes over me, making me want to gag. "Perhaps your name is really Miss Yankee Doodle. How about we settle on Molly Doodle then? Or shall it be Yankee Pitcher?" He guffaws, amused by his own humor. The swell of soldiers grows silent and uneasy.

He calls out to the crowd. "See, we're all parched here, Molly Doodle, every last one of us. Won't you give us a little drink? How about some of that Southern hospitality we've heard about? We ain't seen none of that, nothing but a bunch of rabble-rousers." His eyes glitter with contempt as his grubby hands reach out to snatch the pitcher from me. I recoil, oblivious to the wave of water sloshing onto my apron.

CHAPTER 15
ANOTHER ARMY OF SOULS

Much to my surprise, the insolent soldier doesn't succeed in touching me. A huge dark hand comes from behind and swats his small grimy one away. Now that same hand holds my shoulder in a fierce grip. Despite my initial relief, I'm wary of my new defender. Perhaps I'm just subject to a different tormentor, and we are still quite a ways from the house. There's no telling what desperation could make a soldier do after days, perhaps weeks, of barely any food or drink. If the Regulars are this dehydrated and deprived, then their Negroes are probably even closer to collapse.

My rescuer speaks in an even tone. "Excuse me, sir, please don't mind my interrupting. Mistress Bolling done sent me down here with orders to collect her girl."

I don't need to look; I know this voice well. As the hulking frame of Big Hank steps up beside me, I want to cry with relief.

"Miss Susanna, your momma be needing your help in the big house right away, getting all the vittles cooking. Uh-huh. Yes, ma'am, we got to go."

A murmur of surprise ripples through the crowd, and an uneasy silence follows. The surly Regular's face is flushed, and he glowers at Big Hank with a malicious gleam in his eye. Unflappable as ever, Big Hank stares straight ahead, waiting to steer me toward the big house and safety. After a precarious moment of indecision, the Regular spits on the ground inches from Big Hank's foot, turns on his heel, and storms off into the crowd.

As we shuffle forward again, I'm breathless. Finally in a small voice, I eke out a few words. "Thank you, Big Hank."

"Yes, ma'am," he answers in a cavalier tone, as if he's merely chopped some firewood. With a sideways glance, I detect some tightness around his clenched lips, but in an instant his usual easy smile is back. Sweat drips from his gray eyebrows into the stream of deep grooves lining his leathery face. I should've known it was he.

After what seems like an age, the lengthy procession dwindles down to the seriously injured stragglers. I pray it's all over finally. It has to be. Although Bollingbrook covers a vast hundred acres, it can't absorb any more enemies, and we certainly don't have the resources to feed all these people, even for a few days.

Just as I start to breathe easier, though, an entirely new wave of downtrodden humanity trudges over the crest of the hill. A procession of former slaves begins in earnest, weighed down to the breaking point with huge bundles of gear. Covered in the worst filth I've ever seen, many looked diseased, yet they stumble along with either a crazed or dazed look in their eye. I flinch at the sight, but can't stop myself from gawking. From their anguished expressions, each shuffle they take requires a Herculean effort. Partially clad, they wear bizarre combinations of rags with luxurious silks, presumably plundered from their former masters' wardrobes.

They flood in by the droves, hundreds of these sorry souls

resembling emaciated ghouls. In fact, there are as many as the Regulars who preceded them, perhaps more. In addition to carrying heavy baggage, many stagger along stooped over with bales of wheat strapped to their backs. A scant few ride bareback atop skeletal horses, using every bit of energy to avoid sliding off their mounts.

Within this motley influx, something achingly familiar catches my eye, but I'm not sure what it is. Blinking, I look back at the same spot, but now I don't see anything. I sigh. If something was there a few seconds ago, it had moved on. I rub my eyes, wishing I could wake from this hellish scenario. But there it is again, further up! I peer over at a thin boy stumbling along under an enormous load, but he's on the far side, nearly obstructed by the mass of Negroes. I've seen him before; I know it. In an instant he disappears again, lost in the chaotic swarm. Perhaps I've hallucinated amidst this overwhelming ordeal, but his profile is uncannily familiar. Although I may be delirious, he looks an awful lot like Leroy. I can't swear to it though.

CHAPTER 16

QUARTERING

A s we near the big house, I force myself to stand tall despite wanting to curl up in a ball. I must bury my fears and carry myself as a proud member of the Bolling family. I want Mother to take pride in me, just as I do in her. Holding my head high, I march up the steps on trembling legs, leaving Penny to wait at the bottom.

When I come into the entryway, Mother gives a visible jolt of surprise, and I flash her a fleeting smile. Bending my knee to curtsy to General Cornwallis, I wobble willy-nilly, nearly toppling over sideways.

Mother fixes her eyes on me as if trying to steady me. Then she declares with false cheer, "General Cornwallis has requested to quarter here with his army this evening, and I have obliged." With a placid smile plastered on her weary face, Mother folds her hands and continues her charade. "So let's prepare their accommodations as best we can and serve them a delicious meal, shall we?" Her feigned nonchalance suggests hosting an enemy general and his gigantic army is all part of an ordinary day.

I nod, my heart swelling with pride. Of course, Mother's

too brave to act according to her true status as a prisoner of war. In contrast, I still want to cower like a little girl. Perhaps I'm not as grown up as I thought a few hours ago.

Mother reaches out and squeezes my hand. Much to my surprise, her hand is trembling even more than mine. However, the marked difference between us is her ability to remain steely-eyed when surrounded by captors. I know that my face is pinched, and I'm wide-eyed with terror. Shame on me.

"Lady Bolling, one last request for the moment. Have you any tobacco for my men? That and a bit of ale or cider would do them well after their long march."

"Sir, we have plenty of drink, but no tobacco to offer." Her voice hardens. "Alas, your General Arnold burned our tobacco warehouses full of a plentiful harvest not long ago. Such a pity for you now."

General Cornwallis scowls at the mention of Arnold's name. Apparently he and Mother share one thing in common: their mutual loathing of the Great Turncoat.

Mother continues, making no attempt to curb the bitterness lacing her words. "At the moment we've only our spring saplings. However, with your army treading all over them, they shan't survive the day."

General Cornwallis nods. "Indeed. Thank you, Lady Bolling. I would appreciate a side of yams prepared in the North Carolina style, my favorite dish from that loathsome state."

Mother nods, her face solemn.

"Now I must attend to my duties. General O'Hara shall remain in the residence recovering from his wounds after a valiant performance at Guilford Courthouse. My adjutant will also stay behind to attend to his needs."

Mother and I follow him onto the portico where she

announces in a steely tone, "Dinner shall be served at candle lighting."

Without any acknowledgment, General Cornwallis descends into the swarm of troops. His voice booms, "Senior Staff, report now!"

At last Mother and I are free to exchange raised eyebrows. Despite our seething souls, quartering at Bollingbrook is officially underway.

Mother hisses, "This is such rubbish; the Redcoats have no right to do this, none at all!"

I'm unable to utter a word to describe the maelstrom of my churning emotions. In the course of an ordinary afternoon, my world has been turned upside down. We're now trapped in our own beloved home, captives of the Redcoats for as long as General Cornwallis so desires.

Looking above the troops, Mother stares across the river. "This is the first time I've ever rejoiced that Father is no longer part of this world." Her voice breaks. "Only so he doesn't have to suffer this indignity with us!"

CHAPTER 17
FEEDING AN ARMY

Right away Mother fills herself with purpose and barks out a stream of orders, her voice curt. "First and foremost, we must save Bollingbrook." She neglects to mention that our lives are also in jeopardy, which is all that preoccupies me right now. "Gather all the servants into the barn except those in the kitchen already hard at work. We'll update them later. Penny, check the slave quarters! Big Hank, bring in the gangs that are still out in the fields. Harriet, calm yourself and check the outbuildings, especially the smokehouse and icehouse. Then report to the barn!"

Within minutes of Mother issuing her commands, slaves race into the barn with stricken looks on their faces. Most hug, sob, and moan with unearthly despair, while others pray aloud, drowning out the animals' random clucks and grunts. Once the entire group is assembled, Big Hank slides the doors shut. Instantly it is dim and dusky like early evening, with shafts of light piercing the rough hewn wood. Mother stands in front of the petrified group, her hands by her side in tight fists.

"As you know, a horde of Red-coated locusts has arrived here at Bollingbrook. According to General Cornwallis, they plan to stay for only one night. Pray to God it won't be a minute longer. However, before we begin full preparations for the meal, there are several things I must tell you. As you probably know, years ago Royal Governor Lord Dunmore promised freedom to those runaway slaves who join the British. No doubt when Cornwallis departs tomorrow, he will happily take every willing slave along with him." She bows her head for a moment. "God knows I haven't the power to stop you. If you want to cast your lot with the British, then go in peace."

Big Hank lets out a roar from the back. "I ain't no secret Redcoat lover, and I don't believe they promises! My last name be Bolling, and I be staying here at Bollingbrook or I'm a die trying."

Mother manages a tight-lipped smile. "For those who wish to remain, I thank you. However, I must also warn you. General Cornwallis may very well take you against your will, as he has done time and again in the Carolinas. I shall plead with him to leave you be, but we are more outnumbered than Gideon here. Keep your eyes cast down at all times. Minimize contact with the soldiers without appearing insubordinate. Make it difficult for them to take you unawares. Stay in groups, even while heading to the necessary. If need be, stow away down in the tunnel."

Mother surveys the group, taking the time to make eye contact with every person. "All I ask is that the tunnel remains our secret. Depending on what happens, it may be the only safe place to hide. My plan is simple, and it is this. We must do our best to keep them happy. Since these men are famished, the best way is to feed them and feed them well. " She scans the room again, nodding at each person. "Prepare it all. Without a doubt they shall take whatever remains anyway, so be generous. Spare nothing, neither food nor drink. Cook every herb, chicken, hog, all livestock with any meat on its bones. Make biscuits, hard tack, and Johnny Cake in amounts you've never imagined. Then we shall pray for God's mercy, so they depart like the locusts they are and leave us be." She surveys the room again. "Am I understood?"

The somber group nods.

Out in the summer kitchen, full-fledged panic is already in the air. Slaves are crying and moaning with despair, and praying aloud as they clatter around, gearing up to create an ample spread for a monstrous invading army with no notice. Knives thud on the wooden worktables, dicing up every vegetable whether fresh from the kitchen garden or the root cellar. Others haul enormous buckets to the well to fill the iron cauldrons, a backbreaking load.

The newly-lit fires in the massive hearths smoke and crackle as if they too are protesting the lobsterback marauders. Between the heat and slew of agitated workers, it grows warmer by the second. Several servants mix dough in massive batches, making Auntie Ruth's legendary butter biscuits by the hundreds, while others prepare the yams requested by General Cornwallis, as well as green beans, carrots, and stewed spinach. Still others stir the ingredients for cornmeal spoon bread, my favorite dessert.

Meanwhile, the field slaves slaughter every last hog, chicken and sheep, skewer them on spits, and roast them in the open air. This will supplement the salted hams, bacon, mutton, pork and sausage hanging in the smokehouse, depleting our resources entirely.

It's hard to fathom the state of our twisted world. We have no choice but to prepare a delectable meal for these wicked trespassers, this uninvited legion of enemies. Yet these same Lobsters who demand our every morsel would relish thrusting a bayonet through Stith's heart. I am so filled with rage that I wonder if I'll explode.

CHAPTER 18
DINNER UNDER DURESS

As the sun sets, the members of Cornwallis's Senior Staff saunter into the house without so much as a knock. Not bothering to wipe the thick scum from their grubby boots, they stack their Brown Bess muskets in a precarious pile in the dining room. Although I fancy grabbing one and firing it off willy-nilly, I know it's futile. They'd overtake me before I could even get off a shot. Plus I haven't fired a musket in years. I've never felt so trapped.

Of course, Mother has already devised a plan. "Penny and Harriet, you'll bring in the platters from the summer kitchen. Then wait with them here in the serving kitchen, ready to hand them over. I forbid you both from entering the dining room." She stops and looks them both in the eye without blinking. "Am I understood?"

Although their eyes are wide with bewilderment, they both nod, nonetheless obedient.

Mother turns to me. "Sukey, you shall serve dinner, and I shall assist you as I can, but no one else. The less Cornwallis sees of our servants, the safer they will be. We don't want him getting any notions of taking them for himself. The poor Harrisons suffered enough losses for all of us."

With shaking hands, I carry an enormous platter of steaming roast pork into the dining room. For the first time in years, Mother's fine damask tablecloth covers our mahogany table, and her crystal chandelier is ablaze with tallow candles melting in the oppressive heat. I woodenly move around the table, doling out heaping portions to the repulsive officers seated in our treasured Windsor chairs. Once the tray is empty, I duck out of the room and return with a second platter piled high with thick slices of salted Virginia ham. I trudge among the men, distributing it with my feet dragging like I'm pulling a load of bricks behind me.

Their eyes gleam as they gaze down at the tender meat as if they haven't eaten a proper meal in months. If the rumors are at all accurate, it's true; they're nearly as badly off as our own Continental Army.

As second-in-command, General O'Hara is seated opposite General Cornwallis at the foot of the table, with thick bandages covering both his chest and thigh. However, I still have no idea which officer is Lieutenant Colonel Tarleton. Perhaps he isn't here after all; no one else appears to have any serious injuries.

Clinging to the empty platters, I back into the corner, overcome with awkwardness. I clutch them to my chest, oblivious to the globs of applesauce oozing down onto my apron.

A mustached officer chuckles and elbows the handsome red-headed officer in a green uniform next to him. "Take a gander at this one, will you? A real damsel in distress!"

With a start, I realize he is mocking me. I right the trays, revealing my soiled apron, and feel myself flush to a crimson red. Mortified, I stammer, "Pardon me. I must get back to the kitchen." Rollicking laughter echoes in my ears as the door swings shut behind me.

With tears dribbling down my cheeks, I race out to the summer kitchen, knowing that sweltering, smoky sanctuary will comfort me. Once I lay my weepy eyes on Auntie Ruth's angelic face, I blurt out, "Oh, I've made such a featherhead of myself in there!"

With a crooked smile, Auntie Ruth leaves the fiery hearth and hugs me close. Then she removes my soiled apron and replaces it with a clean one. As she brushes out the wrinkles, her tender touch soothes my soul. "Don't let them rattle you none, Miss Sukey. You doing just fine." She hands me two heaping baskets of warm cornbread drizzled with honey and pats my shoulder. "You bring this in there, and you act like ain't nothing happened. You go on now, you hear? That's all there is to it!"

I nod, blinking back tears. The cornbread's heavenly aroma makes my stomach growl, but for now I must accept my new role. After all, right now I'm a servant too – a slave of sorts to Cornwallis. Returning to that dining room is the last thing I want to do. But I must. Mother is right. We can't risk sending in Penny or Harriet. I couldn't live with myself if Cornwallis took either of them away.

After several deep breaths, I re-enter the room, ignoring their oily smirks and obnoxious snickers. To my surprise, the handsome officer in green smiles at me, his deep blue eyes twinkling.

"No worries, miss. Even Molly Pitcher is entitled to a good daydream once in a while, isn't she?" Enchanted by his lighthearted banter, I flash him a coy grin in return as my neck grows warm. Within seconds, disgust courses through my body for acting as coquettish as silly Betsy. Alas, I'm far worse than her; I actually flirted with the enemy! At least she's no traitor to the cause, but I am. My cheeks feel aflame, as well they should, to reflect my deep shame. I'm just grateful Mother wasn't present for my unpatriotic behavior. I could never make it up to her.

I place the baskets on the table and duck out of the room. I certainly didn't expect any kindness, let alone charm, from a single Redcoat. They're supposed to be cruel, heartless even, like that infamous brute Tarleton, also known as Bloody Ban. After taking a deep breath, though, I return with Mother, ferrying a succession of serving bowls brimming over with yams, carrots, and creamed corn. I do what I must; I have no choice.

Upon serving himself a heaping portion of yams, Cornwallis clears his throat and stands to face his officers with Mother's treasured crystal goblet in hand. "Bless this great bounty before us and the fine hospitality we have received from Lady Bolling. We ask God to guide us tomorrow morning as we embark upon our most important mission of all." He raises his glass in a toast. "God save the King!"

The officers slam the cherished glasses together, shouting in unison, "God save the King!" Silence falls over the room as they tear into the meal, eating every succulent morsel, including the last crumb of cornbread.

Then with a satisfied pat to his belly, General Cornwallis chuckles. "After this delicious meal, I'm tempted to take their kitchen slaves along with us." I stifle a scream just as it rises in my throat. "Those yams were the finest I've had yet in our Colonies, even better than North Carolina."

Mother and I exchange dark looks before she departs the room. He's quite mistaken, but it has nothing to do with Auntie Ruth's delectable yams. The truth of the matter is that the "Colonies" of which he speaks no longer exist and haven't since July 4, 1776. Furthermore, he is an uncivilized brute, leading the infiltration of the Southern states in the sovereign country of America.

Taking pains to keep my face blank, I gather up several empty glass pitchers. Although I don't know what General Cornwallis meant by their "most important mission," it certainly sounded ominous. Surely they've had many objectives of far greater significance than traipsing through rural central Virginia! The Battles of Charleston, Cowpens, Kings Mountain, and Guilford Courthouse are just a few that cross my mind.

I round the table, failing to notice the displaced butt of a Brown Bess that has slid off the pile. Before I know what's happening, I've tripped and fallen to the floor, smashing the pitchers beneath me. Pushing myself onto my elbows, I look down and gasp. My smarting palms are crisscrossed with ruby red scratches pooling blood.

Right away the mustached officer ridicules me, his voice dripping with sarcasm. "Alas, Molly Pitcher has no more pitchers. What a pity. So now she is just Molly. Molly with no pitchers." The others cackle, their guttural guffaws echoing off the blank walls. However, I am heartened to notice there's one exception to this loathsome lot: the handsome officer in green. Putting aside his napkin, he stands, revealing his muscular build, and offers me his left hand with a gallant flourish. However, in a flash I understand why he is unable to offer his right one as well: it's encased in a thick wad of bandages.

So he is the infamous Tarleton! Too shocked to hide my horror, I recoil back from his extended hand. After several awkward attempts to regain my balance, I finally scuttle to my feet. My cheeks feel aflame; they must appear scarlet. Drat! I should've known from the start! After all, he and his villainous dragoons are notorious for their distinctive green uniforms. Then I trot out of the room with their jeers ringing in my ears.

Penny awaits me in the serving kitchen with a sympathetic smile and a broom, just as Mother rushes in with yet another tray from the summer kitchen.

Penny explains, "Mistress, Miss Sukey had an accident, but she be fine. I'll go clean that mess up right quick."

Mother's eyes blaze as her face drains of color, and she rebukes Penny. "Absolutely not! Those swine mustn't see you, not for a moment."

Penny flinches, as do I. Mother's never snapped at her, certainly not like that.

In a calmer voice, Mother continues. "Penny, that would be the end of you here. I have no doubt they'd take you away just like Arnold made off with your brother. It's worth it to me to clean up that broken glass myself, even on my hands and knees."

With her gaze cast down, Penny hands the broom to Mother who lifts her head and shoulders and marches into the dining room as if she is about to win an award. After letting several tears fall to the floor, Penny rights herself. Finding some rags, she bandages my cuts as I wince.

Swallowing my pride, I go back into the dining room and stack up the empty platters, gritting my teeth to offset the stinging in my hands. Mother sweeps up the broken glass, her head bowed.

Cornwallis drones on, his highbrow accent grating on my every nerve. "It's only a matter of time until they succumb. Take heart; we are wearing them down minute by minute. The end is in sight now." He pounds his fist on the table, rattling the glasses. "We've been victorious throughout the entire South! Once we capture Virginia, we will have decapitated the rebels, splitting them in two. Soon we'll divide up these plantations among us." He chuckles and surveys the rooms. "I myself have set my sights on this one."

Lifting his fist to his chin, he ponders a moment. "But

until Virginia is subdued, our hold on the Carolinas will be difficult, if not precarious."

This nightmare of a night continues to wear on. Dear Lord, will it never end? Masking our outrage, Mother and I refill so many drinks of ale, whiskey, and wine that we lose count. Meanwhile Cornwallis rants on, his pretentious voice growing louder and more ornery with each round. Gadzooks, he's more annoying than a donkey braying at dawn.

"We must hunker down somewhere and escape these rabble-rousers and their nasty guerilla warfare for a while. Officers, listen to me when I say Virginia is the ideal place for a permanent camp! Now that I've sent Arnold packing back to New York, I have 3,500 more Regulars at my disposal, bringing us up to 7,000. That more than makes up for any losses from our victory at Guilford Courthouse."

Suddenly the room falls eerily silent, and I'm suspicious. Perhaps his Senior Staff don't consider it such a victory, considering the heavy cost of human lives.

He scoffs. "I'd sooner go to hell than go back to the Carolinas. That is surely the most barren, inhospitable, and unhealthy part of North America. There the gnats devoured us, covering us with welts, while that mud, rain, and sweltering heat about killed us all." He shakes his head as he scowls. "Anything to escape that godforsaken humidity, constant sickness in North Carolina, and the almost universal spirit of revolt. Remember how we went forward? The rebels flew before us. Then when we came back, they would follow us with zeal and bayonets only. They neither fought nor fled, but kept such distance that we were always a day's march from them. We seemed to be playing at bo-peep. It was almost impossible to catch those enemies hiding behind bushes."

His face turns purple with rage, and he pounds his fist on the empty mantle. "And where were all the Loyalists flocking to our banner? General Clinton promised them in droves, more than any other colony. What a load of hogwash! We did nothing but fend off relentless attacks on our supply lines! And that dreaded Swamp Fox, striking at dawn and then disappearing into those infernal swamps like some backwater phantom." His face twists into a sneer. "And I thought New England was the hotbed of this rebellion!"

He marches over to the window and gazes out. "Oh, but at Guilford Courthouse, I never saw such fighting since God made me. The Americans fought like demons. Their amount of resistance was the stuff legends are made of!" He shakes his head. "And that hulking Private, Peter Francisco! He is indeed a one-man army, and what a fearsome one at that!"

Fury returns to his voice. "However, once I have my way, and I shall see that I do, this revolt shall be put down much sooner than anyone would think, even His Majesty."

To conceal my disgust, I keep my eyes glued to the floor and exit the room. Of course his bragging is pure poppycock. There is nothing anyone in sleepy Virginia can do to end this war, not even the mighty Cornwallis. Although his inebriated drivel pains me, I leave the door ajar with my ear cocked as I shake my throbbing hands while awaiting the arrival of the dessert trays. Perhaps a new detail about Guilford Courthouse could shed light on my brothers' fate. If only!

Alas, the evening lumbers on into eternity. To her credit, Mother still wears her stoic smile plastered like a tattoo on her face. Dizzy with exhaustion, I stifle a succession of yawns as my eyelids grow heavy. How I want to escape this horror and curl up next to Mother like a little girl. This is the worst day of my life, other than losing Father and my sisters, and I pray for mercy. It must end soon, or I shall lose my mind.

General Cornwallis's shouting fills the room, reaching a crescendo. I'm willing to bet they can hear him out in the fields.

"Tomorrow holds our sweetest victory! We shall get our hands on the Boy once and for all." He's all but drooling in anticipation.

I had no idea my heart could hold so much hatred.

General O'Hara pipes up. "What became of Arnold's guide? His knowledge of the area made the raid here such a rout." He sneers. "It certainly wasn't Arnold's prowess."

Cornwallis arches his eyebrows. "That confounded Arnold sent the Negro over to the Boy's camp to gather intelligence, but he has yet to return. No worries, we shan't wait an extra moment. Never underestimate the advantage of surprise; its power is too great to forfeit. This is a brilliant opportunity to exploit, no doubt with surefire success. The longer we linger here, the greater the chance of the Boy discovering we are almost upon him. Cheers!"

The men clink their glasses together yet again with a thunder of approval.

"We must quell this dreadful mutiny of bumpkins. Mark my words, my new campaign is the answer to snuffing out this Yankee insurrection for good! Arnold warned me not to step foot in Virginia, but I don't trust him any more than Judas." He smirks. "After all, they both sold their souls for some silver, didn't they?"

The officers erupt into hoots, stamping their grimy boots and slamming their goblets in a discordant symphony.

On the other side of the door, Mother mutters to me, "Dear God, Father's floors shall never be the same."

Cornwallis rants on. "That confounded braggart wanted all the glory for himself. Such hogwash! Virginia is far too important to abandon. After all, it's the largest and the richest! Plus it's the median as well, so here we can cut the Colonies in half. Since the French deliver supplies to the Chesapeake, we shall choke them there. We shan't leave this colony until she is conquered."

"Since General Clinton can't communicate or even decide on a course of action, I have taken it upon myself." He chortles. "Of course, he shan't be cross at all when we've captured the Boy." He beams, already celebrating his surefire success.

"Arnold found Jefferson snoozing in January with nary a shot fired. And so we shall find the Boy equally unaware tomorrow! I shall dislodge him from Virginia and destroy every magazine in the area. Then I will send him off to London in chains. Such humiliation will destroy any remaining French enthusiasm for this costly American War. Finally Louis XVI will stop wasting his francs on these loathsome barbarians! We shall put them down and destroy their preposterous notions of liberty at last."

I'm perplexed. 'The Boy?' But who is 'the Boy?' And why is he so important? In a flash, I recall the men gathered at Joseph's funeral. The Boy is none other than General Lafayette! My mind is reeling. Unless my ears are deceiving me, or my mind is scrambled beyond comprehension, they have a concrete plan to capture him! A scream rises in my throat, but I push it down with a muted cough.

Alas, General Cornwallis hasn't finished his jeering. "That sorry Boy is certainly no match for my British Southern Army. By nightfall tomorrow we shall put him to bed without any dinner." He snickers. "With this decisive victory to come in Virginia, the long insurrection shall be over, and by my hand!" He raises his glass in another toast. "Here, here! To capturing the Boy!"

As I place another abundant basket of butter biscuits on the table, the officers cheer and clink their glasses. Of course, they give no thought to the frothy ale spilling in a mini-waterfall onto Mother's treasured table linens that she inherited from her mother. Their harsh snorts of laughter ring out as anger surges through every sinew of my body.

"We shall take Bon Bon Pants from the derriere!" roars

General O'Hara, raising his glass extra high. He winces and clutches his wounded shoulder, his pain giving me immense pleasure. Again the officers shout their boisterous approval and crash their glasses together.

I'm busy stacking a sea of empty platters when another officer enters the room. Out of the corner of my eye, I see him issue a crisp salute to General Cornwallis.

"Sir, we've just returned from our scouting mission. As you requested, we fanned out across the northern area, and your suspicions are indeed correct. The rebel troops are camped along the north side of the James, probably since General Arnold's last raid. As for the Boy, we've confirmed his location at the Half Way House as best we could. As you know, sir, it is ten miles from here, midway to Richmond and the only stopping place en route. Since it was broad daylight and they had two sentries posted, we could only observe from the edge of the clearing. However, we did spot a white steed at the hitching post, presumably belonging to the Boy."

My head is whirling. Of course, I have no idea what this means. However, it must be momentous to justify interrupting the General's dinner.

A beaming Cornwallis replies, "Excellent research, Captain. You have served His Majesty admirably."

"Thank you, sir. Growing up here in City Point provided me a remarkable advantage."

Curious, I turn to study the officer. Presumably I know him, or at least of him; it's such a small town after all. With but a glance I recognize him, despite the many years gone by. There stands Stith's childhood chum, Thomas Frederick. He and I lock eyes, but neither of us dares to show a reaction. Finally he gives me a curt nod. With a blush, I turn on my heel, duck into the serving kitchen, and listen from there.

General Cornwallis clears his throat. "Indeed, it's only the Boy who insists on riding a white horse, fulfilling his childhood fantasies or some such nonsense." His voice drips with disdain. "I was already an Officer in His Majesty's Army when he was in nappies!

"But with this intelligence, our plan is now firmly locked into place. We shall set out at first light. Mark my words, THE BOY SHALL NOT ESCAPE ME!" He pounds his fists on the table, even startling me in the next room as the wine glasses shake yet again. "The Hound here before you shall outwit that Fox with his silly ploys of deception and false information. When I have the Boy in my clutches, we will have thwarted the Fox in a success for the ages."

Perplexed, my mind churns with endless possibilities. Presuming Lafayette is the Boy and General Cornwallis the Hound, then who, pray tell, is the Fox?

General Cornwallis's voice bursts forth with the force of mortar fire. I'm surprised it doesn't jolt the glasses yet again. "When we capture the Boy tomorrow, our surprise shall surpass the Fox's crossing of the Delaware on Christmas Day!"

Nearly swooning, I finally make the connection. The Fox is none other than General Washington himself! Within a matter of hours, my home has become the nerve center of the war. With downcast eyes, I shiver.

CHAPTER 19
THE BOY IN JEOPARDY

As I enter the room with Auntie Ruth's beloved Indian pudding topped with fresh cream, my stomach gurgles again. It's no wonder; I haven't had anything to eat or drink since this outrageous aggression began.

The mustached officer speaks up. "Sir, how many guards shall we post tonight? The Regulars are standing by awaiting your orders."

"As we are all bleary-eyed from our long march, we shall post only two this evening. The first shall be here at my door. Given your knowledge of the area, Captain Frederick, you shall serve as the second, a roving sentry on the grounds. We have no need for more. No doubt those rabble-rousers in North Carolina are still unaware we've departed their miserable colony."

It takes all my will not to roll my eyes.

"Here in Virginia, their little Navy floats about in paper boats, such a pathetic attempt." He chuckles. "And of course the French boats are far too showy to venture upriver and provide any real assistance to these treasonous rebels."

General Cornwallis pauses to toss back yet another jigger of whiskey. "Rest well tonight, men, for tomorrow shall be a momentous day for our children's history primers!" He pauses. "And then we must find ourselves a deep-water port to send some Regulars back to defend New York City. Our intelligence says General Washington's attack there is imminent."

My heart pounds like I've just sprinted across the length of Bollingbrook. It's a wonder the Redcoats can't hear it thumping. However, I keep my face blank, pretending I've paid no attention. At the first opportunity, though, I leave the room, to find Penny waiting with several peach pies.

She gasps. "Miss Sukey, you hear that? He getting Lafayette tomorrow and putting him in chains!" Her eyes bug out as we stand transfixed, gaping at each other.

I re-enter the dining room with the tray, eager to hear more of Cornwallis's gloating. "The Boy has no way of knowing we're here. After all, even our own Commander-in-Chief doesn't know." Walking over to the fireplace, he rests his hand on the empty mantle and turns to face his staff. "In fact, no one could possibly know of our plan, save for the gracious lady folk here, more likely simpletons than members of a sophisticated network of spies." He raises an eyebrow as raucous laughter ripples around the table. The idea of a provincial widow and her clumsy daughter posing a threat to their brilliant scheme is nothing short of preposterous.

Will this torture never end? Although General Cornwallis's derision doesn't surprise me, I smart from his insult nonetheless. After all, we Bollings date back to the Jamestown Settlement's first families, and Pocahontas and John Rolfe are my great-grandparents. If it weren't for this cruel war, I'd be a grown woman with social standing in my own right!

"Come tomorrow General Clinton shan't be angry when

we have the Boy in our possession once and for all. Then perhaps our King will realize who should have been his first in command from the start." He snickers, impressed by his own cleverness. "But we shan't stop there. Tartleton, you and your men in green shall go capture Jefferson at Monticello and then go onto Charlottesville for their feeble General Assembly. The rest of us shall seek out a deepwater port on the Chesapeake so we can receive supplies and ferry our men back to New York before the Fox invades."

Aghast, I depart the room, not daring to sneak a glance at Mother. The door bumps into Penny pressed against it.

"If they get him, they right. This war be over, sure enough. Uh, huh." She shakes her head. "Yes siree, Miss Sukey. It be over then."

Back in the serving kitchen, Mother and I stare at each other, wide-eyed. Grabbing a candle, she motions toward the cellar. We race down the steps into the darkness and huddle together in the corner. Despite what we just overheard, the momentary distance from the enemy and nearness to Mother soothe my soul, allowing me my first moment of relaxation since the occupation began.

Mother sputters, "That arrogant fool."

I'm taken aback.

"I'd love nothing more than to spit in his pompous face. And I would, too, if it would do any good."

I have no doubt she means it. All I want to do is slink into the tunnel and fall into a deep sleep. My world is unraveling, piece by piece, and I don't have the energy to even dream about fighting back.

Mother moves from anger to despair. "Oh, dear God. What shall we do?" she whispers, wringing her hands. The flickering candlelight exposes her acute anxiety, so well masked upstairs, but which now clouds her face with deep creases. "I've got a mind to head up north and warn General Lafayette myself."

Her notion is ridiculous and thankfully all but impossible. After all, Britain's Southern Army surrounds us on three sides, and the Appomattox contains us on the fourth. Her every movement would be visible to hundreds, if not thousands, of the King's men and escaped slaves. She can't be serious. I pray not, but I'm compelled to reason with her nonetheless.

"But, Mother, there isn't time! Didn't you hear? They're setting out at dawn. They're going to capture him tomorrow. Tomorrow before midday!"

"Oh, there's time all right." Mother frowns with a grim set to her chin. "There's plenty of time for an old woman to take a ride in the moonlight along an old Indian trail."

I gulp at this gibberish. Even before the war, Mother wouldn't allow me to travel on that isolated road during daylight hours by myself. And she's never allowed riding at night, even for the boys. The idea of her heading out there alone in the darkness is absurd. She's daft to even contemplate it.

Oh, it's the bravest of intentions, finding General Lafayette and warning him herself. However, there's no doubt many a soldier would notice her leaving Bollingbrook. She certainly couldn't saddle up at the stable with Regulars covering every inch of ground. Moreover, Arnold destroyed many bridges during the raid; now the nearest one is quite a distance away. In addition, presumably every plantation along the Appomattox is also covered with sleeping Regulars.

My mind sprints ahead. How in God's name could Mother possibly cross the river in total darkness? Even the muted sound of paddling a canoe could attract attention. Of course, swimming poses a grave danger, especially when weighed down by a water-logged petticoat. As I learned as a child, it's heavier than a handful of bricks. Moreover, the pitch darkness would surely disorient her. Even if she somehow made it to the other side, then she wouldn't have a mount! No, although her plan is noble and well-intentioned, it's futile!

The most terrifying possibility of all is General Cornwallis looking to consult with Mother while she's absent. I shudder. I couldn't possibly explain that away, not in the middle of the night. And if they apprehended Mother along the route, they'd hang her. Although soaked in sweat, I shiver. A tingling sensation rises along my spine.

"Never mind. Don't worry yourself, Sukey." Mother interlaces her fingers in mine for the first time since I was a tot. "I know in my heart I can't do it, so don't you fret. There's too much at stake. The Redcoats would surely notice if the lady of the house disappeared for hours, even at night. As distressing as it is, we'll just have to watch history unfold from our side of the river." She releases a defeated sigh. "Losing General Lafayette will end French support and ruin our cause. Aye, there's naught we can do but pray." She frowns down at her chapped hands. "If only we could get word to Peter Francisco. Even injured, I have no doubt he'd set off and find Lafayette, making us all burst with pride once again. But alas, we haven't the time."

My mind scrambles for an answer. There has to be one; we can't give up now! If we don't take action, our cause for liberty is all but doomed. Poof, gone, over! This would be the final blow, crushing our Patriot hopes, dreams, and sacrifices forever.

What would Father say? Just stand by in safety, and let them capture Lafayette? Don't even lift a finger to warn him? I think not. So many others have risked everything for freedom. It's my turn now, petrified as I am.

"But, Mother, there is a way! I should be the one. I'll warn him."

Mother is silent, as if my idea is so preposterous that she can't even process it.

I beseech her. "You must let me do this!"

Her eyes grow wide, and she all but growls at me. "Nonsense, Sukey! You're far too young, and it's much, much too dangerous for a girl like you."

My voice is surprisingly steady despite my tingling body. "But I can do it, Mother! I must, and I'm not that young, not anymore!" By now my heart is pounding so hard I fear it will burst out of my chest.

Mother massages my hand. "It's too much for you, my dear, but you're quite brave to offer."

But I am resolute. "We have no choice! There's no one else to do it."

"I do have a choice, Sukey, and I have chosen no." Mother's voice is cold. "That shall be the end of that."

"Mother, as Patriots, we must get word to General Lafayette. We have to do this! It's our very duty! We've got to do it for the boys, for Father, and for freedom. After sacrificing so much for so long, we can't just let it end like this! We can't sit on our hands while they round up General Lafayette and send him to the gallows. If we don't at least try to alert him, we'll regret it forever." I'm adamant, openly defying her for the first time in my life. "I must go, Mother, I must! That's what Father would want, and the boys, too!"

"Don't you know what this would make you, Sukey? A full-fledged spy! And the Redcoats, do you know what they do to spies? They hang them, make an example for all to see! They won't care that you're an inexperienced babe. You'd be only one thing to them – an arch traitor as loathsome as Lucifer himself. Bollingbrook would become the grandest of bonfires. Everyone would see and smell it from miles away, and Cornwallis would march off every slave, including our Penny, to join his ranks."

I'm speechless. Every nerve in my body is electrified. Even my hair feels like it is pulsating. In a strangled voice, I respond in a measured pace, reasoning as I go. "If all the Patriot boys in America can risk their necks every day for years, then I can risk mine for just one night. Surely that's the least I can do. I'm terrified too, Mother! I'm shaking just thinking about it. But isn't every soldier petrified going into battle? I'm sure the boys are. If we expect them to endure that, then I should endure it, too."

Mother's bleary eyes well up, her first sign of tears since the Redcoats arrived. "You're all I have left in this world, my dear. I've given up both of my boys and sacrificed well beyond that. But this, this I cannot do. I can't bear the thought of losing you. To me, that's worse than losing the war and Bollingbrook altogether." Tears spill over as her shoulders shake. "For years now, I've supported our cause with every breath I take, even before Father died when it was barely anything at all. I've poured forth every ounce of energy from the depths of my soul. But here is where I must draw the line. Let some other mother sacrifice her last child, her only living daughter. I've buried two, and I shan't bury a third. I simply cannot bear it. I'm not so strong, not anymore." She hangs her head as if ashamed of her weakness. "Finally this war has done what it set out to do. I

t has broken me."

After a moment, Mother looks me in the eye. "Sukey, you cannot put your life in such jeopardy. I admire your pluck, but I must forbid you."

Her forcefulness takes me by surprise. Of course I understand her feelings, but I must do this. I have to warn General Lafayette or all will be lost. No matter how terrified I am, it's time to stand on my own. If I want to be treated like a young lady, then I must act like one. I can't hide in Mother's shadow any longer, no matter how much I long to do so.

"Mother, I must do my part. If the boys are still alive, God willing, this may save them! And even if they're dead—" I cut myself short and take a deep breath. I continue, my voice faltering. "And if they're gone, I still need to do this, so they haven't died in vain."

Mother looks away, her melancholy eyes welling with tears. "Very well, Sukey, I can't fight you and Cornwallis's Army, not all at once. As a fellow Daughter of Liberty, I know my obligations. I must give you my utmost support no matter how grave my reservations."

Sweet relief courses through my body. This mission is crucial; Lafayette is America's last and only hope. I can't let Cornwallis extinguish our precious cause without giving it my all to thwart his nefarious scheme. It's time to face my fears; otherwise Patriot defeat is imminent.

As we march back up the spiral stairs, I feel like I'm heading to the executioner's block. My entire body tingles, and suddenly I've never been so awake! It's hard to believe I was stifling yawns less than an hour ago. Finally I have an opportunity to affect the outcome of the war! However, now that it's arrived, well beyond the scope of my fantasies, I'm petrified.

CHAPTER 20
PREPARATIONS

Mother gives me a nudge. "Now, Sukey, go rest for a few minutes. You've got a long night ahead of you. I'll send Penny along to help you dress."

Of course, relaxing will be all but impossible. I appreciate Mother's kindness, though, especially knowing her mixed feelings about my perilous mission which is rapidly approaching.

She gestures toward the British officers. "In the meantime, I'll take care of the loathsome lot of them. Time to top off their drinks again and dole out another round of shots. They shall sleep like the dead tonight," she says with a malicious glimmer in her eye. "I shall make sure of it."

Feigning fatigue, I bid goodnight to the officers. In their drunken states, none of them bothers to acknowledge me, not even Lieutenant Colonel Tarleton, for which I'm quite thankful.

Back in Mother's room, I shut the door, press my back up against it, and release a huge exhale. Finally I feel safe, for the moment anyway. As I glance around, the room seems foreign like I've been gone for months, years even. So much has transpired today, yet the most important part has yet to begin.

I flop facedown onto Mother's bed. Unable to calm down, though, I sidle over to the window to observe the enemy encampment. Aside from the familiar crest of the hill and the stars sprinkled overhead in their regular formation, I no longer recognize the view. It's hard to believe that earlier today leafy tobacco seedlings covered these rolling fields, rippling in the fragrant breeze.

As Mother predicted, the Regulars had trampled the life out of them, crushing them beyond recognition. They've also torn apart miles of our wooden fences for firewood. Now lanterns flicker about like fireflies, and a myriad of campfires glow with dancing orange tongues. Though I know better, I still expect to see white canvas tents dotting the horizon, but there are none. Instead, the Regulars lie out in the open air, sprawling over the fields. There is only one potential divider between one soldier and the next: a tall mound of dirt topped by a mangled tobacco plant.

Penny arrives, carrying an armful of my gowns. After laying them on the bed, she peeks out the window, and turns to me aghast. "All those seedlings done gone to nothing!"

Indeed, it's true. Bollingbrook won't produce any tobacco this year, now for a second year in a row. In a moment of irony, though, I'm grateful Arnold already destroyed our harvested tobacco. Otherwise Mother would burn it herself leaf by leaf before letting Cornwallis make off with it. Surely there are limits to Cornwallis's patience with her brazen attitude, and I don't want to find out where they lie.

With nimble fingers, Penny unfastens the buttons on my gown. Soaked through with sweat, the fabric clings like a second skin, but she peels it off me, little by little. As usual, though, unlacing my tight-fitting stays, bodice, and wire hip cages poses an even bigger struggle. Since even the laces are slick with perspiration, she struggles to gain a firm hold. Naturally my underlying chemise is wettest of all, drenched as if dunked into a washtub. Finally free of it all, I give a weary sigh.

While I root through my gowns, Penny hangs up my dripping clothes. "All that new planting lost already, and I still ain't stopped smelling smoke yet." Her voice becomes petulant. "Now why did Leroy have to go run off and join them like that? It ain't so bad here, not if he didn't make trouble for himself. No telling if he's still alive, and I may never find out neither." She shrugs. "There ain't no use worrying, though, but I can't help it." Of course, I don't dare tell her that I may have had a glimpse of him out there. It's not fair to raise false hopes.

Although relieved to see my black linen gown, I can't help but frown. Unfortunately I've worn it more than I could've imagined when making it. Of course, my first wearing was the most painful by far, burying Mary and her baby. My eyes fill with tears, reliving that heartbreaking farewell. It's been two years, but sometimes the grief is as fresh as if she had just drawn her last breath. Since then, not a month has passed without at least one wearing, usually more. Then just weeks ago, I wore it again to Joseph's funeral.

Wearing my funeral gown tonight is downright morbid. Perhaps it is a bad omen as well. Then again, I'd be a beetle-minded fool to wear anything else, wouldn't I? So much is at stake, the life of America as well as my own. I need the best cover possible; even the moonlight could expose my whereabouts to the enemy. Of course, I haven't owned a riding habit in years, let alone a dark one. However, I must keep faith. I'm resigned; I must wear it. No, I'm not dressing for my funeral. I remind myself this is a prudent decision.

More than anything, I long to skip wearing my heavy wool stockings, but they will help prevent chafing over such a long ride. I don't care what Mother thinks; I won't ride sidesaddle like a demure girl tonight. Sitting balanced on top is safer and more secure. Then I can go at a faster pace and maintain it for longer in the blanket of darkness surrounding me. For once, being ladylike is the lowest of my priorities. Huzzah! Any social faux pas, even if intentional, is unimportant. I smile for the first time since the plague of Red-coated locusts descended upon us.

All that matters is getting my warning to Lafayette and making it back home undiscovered. Thankfully no roosters are alive to crow come morning; the Regulars roasted them, along with every animal they could get their filthy hands on. For once Big Hank won't blow his cow horn to wake the slaves thirty minutes before sunrise.

Without a doubt, though, nary a lobsterback can witness my arrival back at the dock. There would be no plausible explanation, especially to the Commander of the British Southern Army. After tolerating Mother's testiness and giving into her tiresome demands, surely he'd wreak vengeance upon us. Regardless, I must take the risk. Our cause for liberty deserves that and much more.

My tentative plan is risky at best. If the Redcoats expose me as a spy, my neck will be literally at stake. There is no question the butt of a rifle would press against my back, guiding me to the gallows without so much as a trial, most likely with Mother in tow. I gulp back the tears that threaten to choke me. Out of spite, Cornwallis probably wouldn't allow my burial in our cemetery on the bluff. The thought of my body's separation from Father, Sallie, Mary, and her baby girl for all eternity makes me want to sob.

I shiver. If they find me out, they'll hang me without a doubt. However, countless other Patriots have suffered the same punishment. There's no reason I shouldn't be willing to endure it as well. If only I could display the same raw courage as Nathan Hale on his way to the gallows. I mull over his last words, "I only regret that I have but one life to lose for my country." Could I possibly muster such bravery? Alas, I hope so, but I don't want to find out.

Penny shakes my thick hair from my trademark braid, brushes out my long locks, and re-braids it, all without a tug. I pour water into the washbasin, sprinkle some on my face, and pat my cheeks. Of course, I no longer need to revive myself. However, until every last Redcoat is dead asleep, I must do something to occupy my nervous energy.

Next she slips my black gown over my head. For comfort's sake, I insist on skipping my confining stays. Although I'm tempted to avoid my cumbersome petticoat too, my gown already reaches the floor. Extra fabric at the bottom would be an additional hazard. Of all items, though, my black funeral bonnet is key. Hopefully its wide brim of coarse muslin will protect me from the constant onslaught of wayward branches on my ride through utter darkness. Otherwise, they will slash my face to bloodstained ribbons.

Once I'm dressed, Penny heads down to the dock. "Miss Sukey, your mama done told me to make sure your canoe got its paddle waiting and put a lantern in there, too."

Well after ten, Mother returns to the room balancing gnarled apples, ham biscuits, and a cup of cider, with some black garments draped over her shoulder. I'm taken aback; I've never seen her face so drawn and beleaguered.

"What a loathsome bunch of boors! They finally finished up the last of our whiskey, exchanged their slurred good-nights, and staggered off to dream of capturing our dear Lafayette." She scoffs. "I've a good mind to offer Cornwallis a steaming cup of Liberty tea with his grits come morning."

I don't hesitate to chide her, issuing a sharp retort. "Mother, no, you mustn't! You'll jeopardize everything!" I've never criticized her before, let alone scolded her for inappropriate talk. Until now, only Mother has had the authority to reprimand me. I'm already missing those days. Too much has changed in just one day.

She frowns. "Oh, Sukey, I know better than that, but it's certainly amusing to ponder." She places the clothes on the bed. "While they were drinking the last of our precious whiskey, I gathered these from Stith's room." She grins. "Even a proper young lady needn't wear a gown and petticoat tonight."

With a quick draw of my breath, I flash her a nervous smile, comforted by the notion of wearing Stith's clothing. I enlist her help in disrobing and then slip into the shirt and pants.

Next she hands me two overstuffed ham biscuits and the cider. "I know your nerves are up, my dear, but you must eat something. You haven't had a morsel since our invaders arrived." Although I'm in no mood to eat, I oblige her, forcing myself to tear off small chunks and wash them down with the cider. I'm too nervous to chew.

After an excruciating wait, the Regulars finally extinguish their lanterns, and their campfires dwindle to scattered red-hot ashes. At last our intruders are all abed, and it's time to begin my terrifying odyssey. With a wan smile, Mother slips the apples into the pockets of my baggy trousers.

"These are for the horse, and here's Father's compass as well. You'll need it tonight far more than me. Thankfully, Leroy didn't make off with that as well."

My eyes flood with tears. I'm touched that Mother trusts me with such a treasured belonging.

"And I told Penny to put a lantern in your canoe. Remember now, Sukey, don't light it until you're well on the other side! Wait until you have plenty of cover around you!"

I force myself to give a slight nod. I'm hardly brainless; of course I wouldn't do something so obvious to expose myself.

However, I'm far too jittery for Mother's nonsensical advice to rankle me as much as usual. No doubt she's just as anxious as I am.

A chant of, "Spy, spy, spy!" rings in my head, followed by, "We hang 'em high, high, high!" I can already hear the rhythmic pounding of the hammers as the wicked Tarleton directs the construction of a wooden scaffold for the sole purpose of killing me and then reveling in my demise.

"And Sukey, you must return well before sunrise! Heaven help you if they spot you on the trail!"

I freeze, overcome with fear. I hadn't even considered that! Since there's but one road, I can't allow anything to delay me.

"Go ashore at Jordan's Point." Ignoring my quizzical look, Mother continues. "And then take the path on the right to Cousin Elizabeth's farm. It's the closest place to land, and you certainly know it better than anywhere else."

She pauses, leaving unspoken the reason for familiarity. Of course, it's Mary. Her former farm adjoins Elizabeth Bland's with a shared landing.

I used to go there daily to see her. Since losing her and the baby, though, I've avoided going back there. It still remains a raw wound for Mother and me. At this point, Mary's home is all but abandoned. The fields lie fallow, untouched since her husband joined the militia to escape his grief.

"It's best you go that way, Sukey, as hard as it will be for you. Then find Elizabeth's young stallion. He's jet black, perfect for tonight. I believe his name is Raven."

I nod, my hands shaking. It's hard to believe this is really happening. But after all, isn't this what I've craved for so long? It's an opportunity to truly help the Patriots. Now that my chance is here, though, I realize how naïve I was. However, I have no choice. If Cornwallis captures General Lafayette, the war is over. It's that simple.

Without warning, the fate of the Revolution suddenly rests on me! The thought makes my hands tremble all the more. Even in my most grandiose daydreams, I never could've imagined such a situation. Mother, Father, and my brothers have always been the brave ones, not me.

"Remember during the bee how Elizabeth prattled on about him?" Mother smirks. "With her Richard gone for years now, my dear cousin runs on about her horses worse than ever. They're like her children since she hasn't any of her own. Anyway, he's young and just been broken, so he should serve you well, with lots of stamina. If I'm remembering correctly, though, he's perhaps a bit skittish and easily spooked. Or maybe that was one of the others." She puts a hand to her chest. "With the way my heart is pounding right now, I'm not sure of anything."

I shift my weight, stifling my urge to huff. I don't have time for Mother's inane jabbering, not now. Of course, she doesn't realize this is far more annoying than Elizabeth's preoccupation with her horses. Somehow during the tumult of the past few hours, our roles have reversed themselves.

"Mother, I must go!"

Avoiding my eyes, Mother clears her throat. "Well then, let's head down to the cellar, shall we?"

"But Mother, you mustn't come with me. If anyone sees us creeping around together, we'll appear even more suspicious."

With a terse nod, Mother acquiesces. "Indeed you are right, my dear."

My eyes well up with unshed tears. "Mother, I'm going to do my best to make you proud."

She gives me a fierce hug, pulling me in close. "I'm already proud, Sukey, so very proud. Just come back safely. That's all I ask."

I drink in her scent, savoring it for a moment, and then

pull away. After a pause, I turn back. "Mother, what about you? It worries me leaving you here alone with them."

Mother scoffs. "You have far bigger worries than me, Sukey."

"But what if..." My voice trails off. I don't dare verbalize my fears. "What if one of them tries to come in here?" I falter for a moment. "What if they... bother you?"

"Father's old pistol is under the dresser." Mother shrugs and waves her hand. "It's been there for years now. I'll be just fine."

I'm still not satisfied. "Well, before I go, let's at least make sure it's still there."

With a heavy sigh, Mother gives in again. "All right, Sukey, if you insist."

"Yes, I do." How odd. I feel like the parent, no longer the impudent daughter.

Standing at opposite ends, Mother and I push the bureau away from the wall. To my relief, the pistol lies on the dusty floor covered in thick tufts of dust as gray as a squirrel's tail. However, two other smaller items are exposed as well, flush against the wall. Recognizing them, Mother and I gasp aloud. Of all things, it's Mother's missing jewelry, for which she blamed Leroy! Despite the lint on her beloved brooch and silver necklace, they both twinkle in the lantern's dim light.

"For the love of God!" Mother draws her fingers to her lips and stares down. "He must've knocked them behind the bureau when he was bustling about. He was always so rough with things." She shakes her head. "Oh dear me, it never occurred to me to look behind here." She's still fixated as if in a stupor. "That poor boy. I feel absolutely wretched." In slow motion, she bends down and gathers up the jewelry. Frowning, she brushes off the dust.

I've never seen her laden with such regret. In fact, this is the first time I've ever seen her question herself.

"Well, there isn't much to do about it, Mother." My voice is barely audible. "He's gone for good now."

"I suppose you're right." She shakes her head as if trying to shake off her self-disgust. "Sukey, one last thing, and then you must go. If they manage to stop you..." Her voice falters, and she raises a hand to her chest. "I can't bear to think of you in such danger." She forces herself to take a deep breath. "But if anybody stops you, tell them you're off fetching a doctor from Richmond." Her voice trembles. "Because your sister's in grave trouble birthing her child." Alas, she is borrowing from the heartbreaking circumstances of Mary and her babe. Mother gives me a baleful glance as her slate blue eyes brim with tears. We both know the truth, though. When a baby's head is too large to pass, there is precious little even the best doctor can do.

I open the door and tiptoe out, wincing as it creaks shut. I'm too scared to look back at my mournful mother for fear I'll lose my nerve. Clad in Stith's clothing, I tiptoe down the dark hallway carrying my shoes and bonnet, with the apples and Father's compass stuffed in my pockets.

CHAPTER 21
READY OR NOT

Dead quiet reigns on the first floor while muffled snores drift down the stairs, presumably from Cornwallis's guard. I hope that bodes well for my upcoming mission. Once I make it to the serving kitchen, I am scampering toward the stairs when a shadowy figure blocks my path.

I freeze. Alas, the dreaded Redcoats have thwarted me before I've even left the house. How pathetic. I'm already a failure before even starting out on my quest. Surely I'll disappoint Mother as well as Father's spirit looking down on me.

The figure speaks in a throaty whisper. "Miss Sukey, it be Harriet."

I release a deep exhale as my pounding heart slows from a full gallop to a mere canter.

"Miss Sukey, forgive me! I done gave you a start, but I'm in fits of worrying for you. I heard Mistis telling Penny." She stifles a sob. "I just want you to stay here, safe with us. That French man can take care of hisself."

I engulf her in a hug and then descend into the utter blackness of the cellar without a word lest I break out in sobs. When another dark shape moves in my direction, I wonder if my imagination has gone crackers. But no, a creature is lumbering toward me, and I stifle a shriek.

"It's just me, Miss Sukey!" Much to my relief, the alarming creature is none other than Penny. "I stayed down here to see you off!" At this point I want to collapse in a fit of hysterical giggles at the irony of it all. An entire army of Redcoats swarms our plantation, yet Penny and Harriet have spooked me before I've even set foot in the tunnel. So much for my fanciful notions of bravery! I so want to tell Penny that Mother and I found the missing jewelry, but there isn't time. Every second of every minute counts. Daylight will be my death knell.

With a deep breath I walk through the tunnel out to the dock. Although the river is as recognizable as my washtub during the day, in the pitch darkness it's become a foreign land. Thankfully the moon provides some dim guidance as the stars twinkle overhead. Gripping both sides of the canoe, I step in gingerly, sit, and push off.

Although heading straight across the river is the shortest distance, it would be pure folly to take that route. The marsh on the other side extends far into the river and surely would bog me down. Wading to shore would make too much noise. So I let the current carry me downriver for a spell. When marsh grass rubs against the hull, I push off and drift downriver a bit longer. Then I paddle toward the other side, spotting the tree limb hanging over the water where Stith and I spent many afternoons jumping in. Anticipating the landing point coming up in a minute or two, I force myself to relax and savor the moment.

Suddenly a floating log smacks hard against my canoe, sending it into a tailspin, and then heading in the wrong direction. I grit my teeth; I haven't time to waste, especially so early in my journey. Thrusting my paddle in the water, I regain control but pass by the landing. After turning the canoe, I paddle my way back against the current. However, once I manage to land, the thick mud sucks at my shoes, requiring me to dislodge them with every step. Finally I pull the canoe high onto the riverbank and make sure to grab the lantern and tinderbox. Paddling my way back upriver in the wee hours of the morning will be a daunting task, especially given my exhaustion by then. Hopefully the darkness will mask my inadvertent splashes as I battle the current.

I push that worry from my mind. I'll deal with it when I must. I have far too many immediate troubles, like finding my way through this blinding darkness to the barn.

Of course, Mother was right. I've landed there countless times to visit Mary, including the day she died. However, nothing looks familiar now. Engulfed in this suffocating blanket of darkness, I could be anywhere.

Once I am well behind some brush, I light the lantern after several attempts with my shaking hands, and set off along the winding path toward the Blands', fingering Father's compass in my pocket.

The tree branches overlap, forming a canopy that rustles in the slight wind. Gazing up in the hazy moonlight, I can make out their crisscrossing outline. Holding the lantern aloft, I walk down the overgrown path, drinking in the scent of damp earth and rotting wood. Low-hanging tree limbs snap against my body like tiny hands grabbing at me, but I press on. Unfortunately, branches are the least of my worries.

As I approach the outline of the darkened barn, a menacing growl rumbles low and guttural from a distance. When the animal charges toward me, I stifle the urge to scream. In the light of the lantern, I see an enormous dog with his upper lip curled back, revealing long straight teeth. Although not normally afraid of dogs, I worry he will rouse Mistress Bland and delay my departure.

"Shhhh!" I hiss as the dog barks with no signs of calming down. Fishing around in my pocket, I toss him an apple. He catches it in his mouth and wanders off to eat his prize without a backward glance. I pray that any future pursuers will be as easy to placate.

I hold the lantern aloft and look around the barn, finding Raven with his sleek black coat in the corner stall. Making my way over to him, I coo and pet his lush mane with short, soft strokes. He snuffles several times in his sleep until finally his eyes flicker open. Raising his head, he pricks his ears in my direction and turns to look at me. Keeping his lips closed, he nickers softly. I can't help smiling at this friendly reception. Oh, we shall make a fine pair after all! As much as it pains me, I have to admit that yet another of Mother's suggestions has been helpful.

For several precious minutes, I pat and caress Raven. After all, I must have his utmost trust for my risky mission to succeed. As I harness him, he tosses his mane, still struggling to wake up. Once outside, I walk him in several brisk circles and then blow out the lantern. Thankfully, there's ample moonlight.

I mount him and slide into the saddle. "Raven, we're going on the ride of our lives! Time to fly!" As I tap him with my heels, he lets out a loud whinny. "Shhh! We mustn't wake your mistress; we have no time to explain."

In my zeal to get to the Half Way House as fast as possible, I'm tempted to keep him at a full-out gallop for the entire trip. If only he could sprout wings and fly like Pegasus from the Greek mythology that I studied so long ago. However, I know better than that; he'll actually cover more ground if I keep him to a steady trot, even with added breaks to walk. The entire route is about a twenty mile round trip. Ideally, though, a rider should change horses after ten to fifteen. However, the young and virile Raven should be able to handle this extended trip. I shall find out for sure, no doubt.

And so, we set out on our quest at a moderately fast pace. I clutch the reins close to my chest, causing the fresh cuts on my hands to smart. Ignoring the pain, I crouch forward, pressing my knees together as Raven's legs move rhythmically in diagonal pairs. I am so thankful for the many times I rode this path years ago with Stith. In the blanket of darkness surrounding me, though, an eerie stillness envelops the trail. I feel as if I'm alone on an alien planet where no man has gone before.

As we make our way north, Raven settles into a steady two-beat gait. I post up and down with his steps, our joint cadence putting me at ease. It's hard to believe this desolate stretch of Indian trail-turned-road is so vital, the only stretch connecting the north with the south.

Within minutes, sweat blankets my torso as I pine for an ordinary day at Bollingbrook, however dull that might be. But no, after years of griping about my inability to contribute to the cause, now is the time for boldness. I must ride like my brothers' lives depend on it, and they very well could. Those words pound through my head, over and over again. They very well could; they very well could; they very well could.

Of course, I must deliver the message to General Lafayette or the unthinkable will happen – his capture. Without a doubt, we'd lose our vital French support, striking the fatal blow to our cause. Despite the nerve-wracking scenario, I owe it to every Patriot soldier from Georgia to Massachusetts. For years they've faced overwhelming odds with utmost bravery, suffering in countless ways, and willing to sacrifice everything.

Finally, I've got the opportunity to achieve something of real significance. This ride is the most dangerous thing I've ever done, but by far the most important. Perhaps the Redcoats are winning, but the war isn't over yet!

Gritting my teeth, I whisper, "Well, Raven, if this be treason, let's make the most of it! 'Give me liberty or give me death.'" Buzzing with adrenaline, I want to shout it out with the conviction of Governor Patrick Henry, but I can't risk drawing any attention, even in my desolate surroundings.

Poor Raven cannot see the trail ahead other than by moonlight, which the overhanging trees make even more elusive. Although his other senses have adjusted to compensate, he can't help drifting from side to side. Smack! A thick branch strikes me on the forehead just below my bonnet, tossing me back in the saddle. Dazed, I gingerly touch the area, and my fingers encounter an oozing sticky wetness. A small knot has already formed there and throbs like it has its own heartbeat. Overcome by a spell of dizziness, I bring Raven to a halt, giving us both a chance to collect ourselves.

As we set off again, I focus my energy on keeping Raven centered. Thankfully the trail is mostly straight and flat. After a bit I relax, savoring the cool night air blowing against me. I picture Paul Revere on his Midnight Ride back in 1775, calling out, "To arms! To arms!"

Then without warning, something flies into my mouth. Egad! It's alive and moving. Although repulsed beyond measure, I keep riding. I can't afford to stop again so soon or I'll never make it back home before sunrise.

Holding the reins in one hand, I fish out the wiggling creature with the other, ignoring my ragged nails scratching my tongue in the process. Despite the enveloping blackness, I have no doubt the creature is a bright green cankerworm; they're out in full force these days. Even during daylight, they're difficult to spot dangling from trees by their invisible silken threads. Thus it's altogether impossible come night-time. However, I'm determined not to endure that repulsive experience again or, even worse, swallow an entire worm. Raven and I lumber on as I tuck in my chin and press my lips together.

After a long spell, thankfully without incident, Raven lets out a squeal and stops short. Taken by surprise, I nearly catapult over his head. He leaps sideways into the brush as I cling to him, my chafed thighs pressed tight. I force myself to use a calming voice.

"What's wrong? What is it, Raven?" I have no idea what danger is lurking, but no doubt something is amiss.

There's an unmistakable rattling sound, and I shiver. Jumping off the horse on the far side, I lead him away into the brush, giving the snake room to retreat. After a few hair-raising minutes, the rattler fades off into the distance. Guided by the moonlight, I lead Raven back to the trail.

We've just gotten back up to full speed when Raven stops short again. Hearing nothing unusual, I peer into the darkness ahead of us, spotting a fallen tree blocking our path.

"Well, this explains it, Raven. Good instincts, my boy." As I stroke his nose, my heart pounds as I try not to think about the perils we've averted and the dangers that still await us.

CHAPTER 22
ARRIVAL AT THE HALF WAY HOUSE

At long last the narrow trail expands into a clearing. I've done it! Euphoria floods through my body. After hours of sharp branches lashing at me from all angles, I've emerged from this ghostly forest intact. The outline of a two-story clapboard building looms ahead. Ah, finally I've made it to the Half Way House!

"Huzzah, Raven! We're free from danger now!" I mutter between heavy breaths. We're now among fellow Patriots, safe at Lafayette's headquarters! Surely the worst is over. Now all I have to do is relay my message and head back to Bollingbrook. My role in thwarting Lafayette's capture is near completion.

Slowing Raven to a walk, I stroke his mane, foamy with sweat. Within seconds his perspiration coats my hand, making it slick. I hastily wipe it on my baggy pants. That is the least of my worries.

Leaning into his sodden cheek, I give him a smooch. "You've done it, my boy. You've served our young country well."

In the distance, a spark flashes and expands into the flickering glow of a lantern. A man calls out in French and then switches to English.

"Qui va la? Who goes there?"

Then a second voice, this one American, bellows out a warning. "Identify yourself now or we will fire!"

Still winded from my harrowing ride, I am shocked by this hostile reception. I lick my chapped lips. My voice trembles as the words tumble out in a short burst.

"I'm Susanna Bolling. I must see General Lafayette right now!"

The tall grass rustles as the guards approach, glaring at me with squinted eyes. I stare back, my sides heaving and heart pounding.

The American sneers at me. "Well, well there, missy. Aren't you an impudent one, demanding to see the General in the dead of night? And to what do we owe this honor? Wouldn't you be better off at home asleep?"

Without allowing me any time to respond, the Frenchman barks, "From where have you come?"

Nerves overcome me; I can't speak. Then, despite my parched and gritty mouth, I finally manage to spit out a response.

"City Point, across the Appomattox." Arching my aching back, I finger Father's compass deep within the pocket of Stith's pants.

"That's quite a ways from here!"

Anger surges within me. Of course, I know it's a long distance! I just traveled it alone in the middle of the night. I want to let out a howl, but instead I bite down hard on my lip. Within seconds, the metallic taste of blood fills my mouth.

The American takes charge. "Now off your mount there, Joan of Arc."

"Aye." I oblige, fuming to myself. Taking one foot from its

stirrup, I lift my leg over the saddle, grimacing as my thighs scream out in agony. Undeterred, I hop to the ground as my overworked legs shake like a newborn foal's. I stagger a few bowlegged steps forward. Unfortunately my shoe catches on a root, twisting my ankle. With a yelp, I sink to the ground in a heap, my eyes filling with bitter tears. Wincing at the blinding pain, I struggle to stand up.

"Come forward now, mademoiselle," the French guard commands in halting English. I take a wobbly step forward, dragging my throbbing ankle. "Now, why is it you come here? These woods hold too much danger for you."

I inhale, attempting to keep my fury at bay. With every minute wasted by these shenanigans, sunrise will arrive even sooner.

"But I must speak to General Lafayette at once! His safety and our cause depend on it!"

Leaning forward, the American hisses at me, all but assaulting me with a wave of his foul breath. "It's the middle of the night. Can't your bit of gossip wait until morning?"

Fuming, I shake my head, refusing to acknowledge his condescension. In an instant my fatigue vanishes, replaced by a boiling rage surging through my body. How dare they brush me aside like a stupid girl! Even if they don't respect me, my message couldn't be any more important!

"Just give us your message, *ma chérie*. We'll be sure get it to him." The Frenchman snickers as the American snorts.

I didn't come all this way for such disrespect. I've had more than my fill from the Redcoats. Although I'm so pressed for time, trusting them is not an acceptable option. Their delivery would come too late, if at all. Needless to say, the stakes are far too high.

"But I have secret information straight from the enemy! Time is running out! I must inform General Lafayette at once."

"So what's the news, miss?" The American shakes the lantern to prod me to speak up. "We'll tell the General when he wakes up. He went down for some shut-eye not long ago."

I let out a shriek. I can't contain my frustration any longer, not after all I've endured.

"No! It can't bloody well wait! They'll capture him by then!" I don't have another moment to waste with these ignorant naysayers. Like Captain John Paul Jones said, I have not yet begun to fight!

A groggy voice with a pronounced French accent floats out an open window. "*Qu'est-ce qui se passe?*"

I can't remember what that means; any French I once knew has long faded from my mind. However, I'm elated to have someone else's attention, hopefully a high-ranking officer.

The guards stare at each other, nonplussed.

After a pause, the voice calls out again in a more authoritative tone. "Who's out there? Guards!"

The American responds. "Yes, General. Everything is under control. We will give you a full report in the morning."

My heart races at a sprint. Apparently I've found my way to General Lafayette himself, but they still won't let me relay my message. This is a cruel complication that I hadn't even contemplated! Refusing to hold back my indignation, I burst out in a loud voice.

"But, General Lafayette, sir, please, I must speak to you at once! I have an important message! It can't wait, or they'll capture you this morning!"

"Ah *bon*, it has been far too long since I've heard the delightful voice of a young lady." General Lafayette has an amused lilt to his voice. "Or perhaps I am just in the midst of a wonderful dream." A low chuckle follows.

Although Lafayette is known for his playfulness, I must make him understand my urgency. "General Lafayette, this can't be any more serious! Your very life depends on it, and the future of America as well! There's no time to waste; they're coming for you at daybreak!"

"What is thees, *mademoiselle*? And who are 'they?' What could be so very urgent at this hour?" A flash of light morphs into a flickering candle in the window. I make out the dim profile of a tall, thin man peering into the darkness.

I can't contain myself any longer; this is no time for etiquette. "Cornwallis is coming for you, sir!"

"No worries, ma cherie. I think not. He remains down at Guilford Courthouse, licking his wounds from his supposed 'victory.'" He laughs into the night air. "I doubt he can afford many more such victories, *oui? Quel dommage*, such a pity! Our men must've enjoyed shooting his horse out from under him, eh?"

"But no, General, no! He arrived in Virginia yesterday with his entire army; he's just across the Appomattox! Please, I must speak to you at once!"

"As you wish, *ma chérie*. I can never refuse a lady." His tone remains lighthearted. "I shall be right down. Guards, escort the *mademoiselle* inside, *s'il vous plaît*, and attend to her mount."

I let out a pent-up sigh. Before last night, I could never have imagined meeting America's beloved General Lafayette, let alone demanding to report to him as an undercover spy in the wee hours of the morning. Finally, I can expose the imminent danger of Cornwallis's scheme before it's too late.

With an irritated grunt, the guards escort me down into a stale basement, leaving me with a lone candle to survey the craggy brick walls, carved wooden fireplace, and stately grandfather clock. By this point my backside is so tender it feels like one massive bruise. Gingerly I lower myself onto a chair at a makeshift table littered with maps and scrolls of coarse paper.

A few minutes later, a slender man with a heart-shaped freckled face and ruddy cheeks saunters down the stairs. Despite being a bit bleary-eyed, he wears a ruffled white shirt and a crimson sash. Although still matted from sleep, his receding red hair is pulled back in a hasty ponytail, displaying his wide forehead and long straight nose.

His youthfulness shocks me. He doesn't appear any older than Alexander. Although I remind myself that he's only 23, I'm still taken aback. After all, he's a Major General in the Continental Army! Despite the early hour, his bearing is aristocratic with the graceful movement of his elongated limbs.

From under arched brows, his big hazel eyes study me. Suddenly his delicate mouth breaks into a boyish grin as he steps forward, kissing me on one cheek and then the other. "*Enchanté, mademoiselle*." His flamboyant gallantry and polished manners charm me. I can't help blushing despite my churning innards and aching limbs. "Now tell me who you are, *s'il te plaît*. What could possibly bring you all this way now, in the middle of the night?"

As the clock chimes, I rush to answer. "I am Susanna, Susanna Bolling, and I'm from City Point, sir, Bollingbrook Plantation. I must tell you..."

General Lafayette interrupts me. "Now, *ma chérie*, slow down *un peu, oui?* I still struggle with my English. I only learned it on the voyage over here. You are quite lucky to find yourself alive right now. Yes, I know City Point quite well. Much to my chagrin, we had to fire upon it to get Arnold to leave. But how did you find your way here? And pray tell, who accompanied you on such a dangerous trip?"

"I know the trail from riding with my brother long ago. I came by myself." I shrug. "There was no other choice."

Lafayette's eyes widen as he cocks his head. "*Incroyable!* All that way, alone? *Mon dieu!*"

Desperate to move past the niceties, I can't wait any

longer. "I had to find you before it's too late. You must leave right now!"

"*Bien sûr! Mais pourquoi?* But why?"

"Sir, I must tell you, it's the Redcoats!" I sputter, spitting the words out. "They're here! They're in City Point! At Bollingbrook! They're moving north at dawn! He knows exactly where you are, and they're all coming to get you!"

"*Mademoiselle*, I am quite baffled." Lafayette furrows his brow and pinches his lips together. "My most reliable source reported Arnold's departure as a *fait accompli*. Hasn't he been sent packing to New York, *oui?* However, perhaps their plans have changed. If so, that is indeed cause for concern. So Arnold is still here, is he, with his merry band of American deserters?" He chuckles. "Ah, I presume he's anchored at Westover again, enjoying the fine hospitality of Mistress Byrd!" He winks with a mischievous smile.

"But, sir, it's Cornwallis who's here now! He sent Arnold back to New York and then took command of his troops. He's got 7,000 men now, spread all over City Point. They're setting out at daybreak, the whole lot of them, General Lafayette! You'd best be on your way right now!"

"*Quelle horreur!*" General Lafayette runs his hand through his ponytail. "So Cornwallis is prowling around Virginia now, is he? That is indeed a surprise, giving up on North Carolina just like that." He gives his fingers a snap.

The words gush out of me. "The Patriots down in North Carolina cut off their lines, so they're exhausted and out of supplies! They're a pitiful lot right now!"

General Lafayette shakes his head with a mournful smile. "We too have a want of supplies. There are soldiers without clothes or boots, soldiers without pistols, soldiers with pistols but no bullets. There are dragoons without swords, horses without saddles, bridles, or boots. There are those with no horses at all." He chuckles. *"Mon dieu,* there is a shortage of everything but shortages!"

I'm crestfallen. After all this time, has General Lafayette given up hope? Has he lost faith in our cause?

Seeing my consternation, he reaches out and touches my arm. "Fret not, *ma chérie!* But the harder the conflict, the more glorious is the triumph. If our rebel warfare has made them so despondent, then they shall have more of it! The Oneida Tribe taught me their tactics at Valley Forge. Rest assured, we shall be more loathsome than all the bugs and heat in Carolina combined!" He chuckles. "Bon Bon Pants, as they so childishly call me, shall teach them a lesson about underestimating the enemy."

Lafayette grins. "The roads are only wide enough to march in twos." He waves his hands in the air. "We will snap at their heels, skirmish, and then withdraw. We must keep them marching, sweating, and hungry. We shall continue to wear them down and win this chess game yet." He beams as his eyes crinkle with glee.

Words bubble up from my chapped lips. "But, sir! There's more I must tell you! Once they've got you, Colonel Tarleton and his Raiders will head west to Monticello to capture Governor Jefferson and the General Assembly in Charlottesville! The rest will head east to Chesapeake Bay to look for a deep-water port to send soldiers to New York and get provisions. They're convinced General Washington will attack there soon."

"Ah, *bon!* We must get word to Governor Jefferson right away. He and the General Assembly are in grave danger. We certainly cannot allow Cornwallis to capture the author of the Declaration who is also Virginia's Governor!"

I grit my teeth. "But, sir, you're first! They're coming for you now! Take heed; you must depart quickly! Cornwallis is determined to catch you by surprise. To make haste, he's burned their baggage, wagons, and tents. He even smashed the hogsheads of rum! Aren't you worried?"

"*Mais oui, ma chérie*, I am quite concerned! *Bien sûr*, I am dedicated to this glorious cause, but I am devilish afraid of him. Cornwallis is much wiser than the other generals. He inspires me with a sincere fear, and his name has greatly troubled my sleep. This campaign is a good school for me. God grant that the public does not pay for my lessons. My only regret is not capturing that despicable Arnold. Alas, he managed to slink off again, just like at West Point. However, I find solace in having saved Richmond from destruction."

"But, sir, you must be on your way now. Last night at dinner, he toasted your capture! He vowed 'the Boy shall not escape me!' I heard it with my own ears!"

Lafayette's eyes twinkle. "Ah *bon!* Watch as I prove him very wrong. Mark my words, *ma chérie*, the hunter shall become the hunted. That Hound shall not escape the Boy! I shall lead him on a merry chase." He winks as his mouth curves into a mischievous grin. "Don't worry, he shan't get the best of me. We shall soon head north to meet reinforcements from Pennsylvania.

"When we are not able to do what we wish, we must do what we can." His face grows serious. "Above all, we must remain patient. In all honesty, were I to fight a battle, I would be cut to pieces. Were I to decline fighting, though, the country would think we'd given up. I am therefore determined to skirmish, but not too far. We can't beat them, but we can exhaust them. A powerful French fleet with 3,000 men will soon arrive from the West Indies, so we must bide our time. Like His Excellency General Washington, I shall not despair. Tyranny, like hell, is not easily conquered. My ancestors fought in the Crusades and later with Joan of Arc; I am equally proud to fight alongside General Washington."

As the clock chimes again, a Negro man enters the room

and sits next to Lafayette. His shaggy beard strikes me as somehow familiar, but perhaps I'm just delirious by now. Although my focus should be on Lafayette, I wrack my brain, trying to place this man. If he's from Prince George County, perhaps I've seen him at the trading station, a funeral, or even a bee. I certainly haven't gone anywhere beyond that realm in ages. However, I've seen him somewhere, though, and I'm sure it was recently.

"James, *mon ami,* would you please bring this young lady a pint of cider and attend to her wounds?" My heart swells with gratitude, although at this point my thirst and bruises are the least of my concerns.

The Negro fetches me the drink. I swill it down with gusto; no liquid has ever tasted quite so delicious. Once I'm finished, I emit an embarrassing burp and feel my cheeks redden. With a wink, he holds up a wet rag and declares, "Now, I'm gonna get you cleaned up here, Miss."

Recognizing that distinctive gravelly voice, I welcome the opportunity to study him up close. Prickles run from the nape of my neck to the small of my back. Oh yes, he's indeed from my area. More importantly, he's also a Redcoat! He's none other than Arnold's guide from the raid! And here Lafayette and I sit, just inches from him, sharing secrets no less! He's a spy no doubt, reporting our every move back to Cornwallis. A wave of fury overwhelms me. Oh, he's the swine of swines!

My entire body shakes. Despite my stiffened muscles, I rise to my feet in one fluid motion, knocking my chair over without regard for my throbbing ankle.

"General Lafayette, I must speak to you at once, alone! You are in the gravest of danger!"

The Negro extends his hands toward me and waves them. "Miss!"

Startled, I recoil.

"Miss, I know what you thinking. We done seen each other in City Point, down at the wharf."

"Yes, I know you, and I know what you really are!" Venomous anger surges through my body. I feel like I'm on fire. "You're a spy!" I spit the words out at him like musket balls.

In a gentle voice, General Lafayette interjects. *"Mademoiselle,* do not be alarmed. *S'il te plaît,* let me explain. First, I commend you. Your instincts are excellent, better than most of my soldiers." He grins. *"C'est vrai.* It is true -- he is a spy for the Brits. But he is a very bad one, feeding them false information and sharing their secrets with me." He shrugs. "Such a pity." He chuckles. "Luckily for us, he has become our most valuable spy. James has learned so much in such a short time."

Still unable to contain my outrage, I huff. "But, sir, he let Arnold burn all our tobacco! Why, he even led him there. He showed him the way!"

James frowns as his eyes sadden. "Yes'm, I done that, and it warn't easy. It broke my heart, seeing all that fine Virginia tobacco go up in flames. You see, the more they think I'm on their side, the more I can find out." He tilts his head toward me. "But don't forget I done told you to save that ammunition at the courthouse! Didn't you wonder why I done that?" He gestures to General Lafayette. "But the General here, he know my every move."

Lafayette's pointed chin bobs in agreement as his eyes glint with amusement. "This was all my plan actually. I recruited him to crossover to them and spy for us, posing as a runaway slave. Huzzah! Then it got even better when Arnold asked him to spy on us. And *voilà*, we've kept them fooled." He raises his index finger. "Ah, do not underestimate the Boy!"

I let out a deep exhale. So it's true. James really is a double spy, but his loyalty is to the Patriots! But I'm still not satisfied; I need to know more. "But who are you? Did you really run away?"

"My name be James Armistead, and I belong to William Armistead over in New Kent County. He loaned me out to help General Lafayette."

"Have you met another Negro named Leroy? He escaped from us during the raid."

"Miss, I never see any Negroes. I always right by Arnold's side, every minute. But they got lots of them, too many mouths to feed."

The clock chimes yet again. "Alas, I must return home before sunrise. Pray tell, may I ask you about my brothers? My mother and I haven't received word since Guilford Courthouse. We're beside ourselves with worry. Just to know their hearts are still beating, even if wounded, would soothe our souls beyond measure."

General Layette nods his head in sympathy. "*Ma chérie, bien sûr*, we shall find out all we can."

"Sir, I hasn't told you yet!" James jumps to his feet. "Just after you gone to sleep, we got a messenger in from Guilford."

"Well then, rouse him right away, James. Let's find out if he knows anything about her brothers."

When I blurt out their names, James's bloodshot eyes widen, and he looks flummoxed. "Did you say Stith? Stith Bolling, is that right?" I nod as he strokes his stubbly chin. "He be a Captain? In the cavalry?"

I hesitate and nod. "Why, yes, he's a Company Commander for the First Continental Light Dragoons."

James beams. "I got to fetch the messenger. You can ask him all about your brother."

Fewer than five minutes later, he returns with a tall, gaunt Captain trailing behind him, wearing our Virginia colors: a dark blue coat with red lapels and lining. As he rubs his eyes with his fists, I'm aghast. It's Stith! The messenger is Stith himself!

"Stith! Is that you?" Incredulous, I put a hand to my mouth. No, this can't be possible, but it's a wonderful hallucination. "Is that really you standing there?"

Still groggy, Stith juts his head forward and stares at me, his eyes puffy and red-rimmed. "Sukey! Gadzooks! How in the world are you here? I must be dreaming!" He grabs me in a fierce hug, knocking the air out of my lungs.

After a moment I pull back. "It's Cornwallis, Stith! He came to Bollingbrook yesterday to quarter! Mother and I overheard him at dinner. He plans to capture General Lafayette this morning. Someone had to come and warn you all!"

Perplexed, Stith is at a loss for words. "How? How in tarnation did you get all the way here? And who came with you?"

I blurt my response in one breath. "Once the Redcoats were finally asleep, I canoed across the river, went to the Blands and took a horse."

But I too have so many questions that I hardly know where to start. "And you! You're a messenger now?"

"Well, we found out Cornwallis was headed north, but no one knew where. They sent me since I know the area. Hopefully anyway." He grins. "So I took the long route, riding west, then north, and heading back east to finally get here." He looks stricken. "I can't believe the louse is at Bolingbrook. How is Mother? Is everyone all right?"

"Yes, we're faring well, so far anyway. We'll only know for sure when he departs. It pains me so much, Stith, but I must head back right away. But first tell me, what of Alexander?" I can only draw in shallow breaths, making me pant. "Please tell me he survived Guilford Courthouse!"

Stith nods. "He did indeed. He came down with dysentery

two days before, so he never made it into the battle at all."
He stifles a laugh. "Of course, he's grateful to be alive, but
quite chagrinned as I'm sure you can imagine."

A spontaneous giggle escapes my lips. "Oh, praise the high
heavens! I can't wait to tell Mother. She'll be so relieved,
dysentery and all."

As the guards stand by with Raven, General Lafayette
bids me farewell, bestowing a kiss on one cheek and then the
other. "Bravo, *ma chérie, bon travail!* You have done your duty
for America and done it very well. If it wasn't for you ladies,
we'd never keep fighting!"

"Thank you, sir, but why do you say such a thing?"

"Why, you Patriot ladies, *bien sûr*! Your dedication is
exemplary. None of the soldiers could bear to look you in the
eye and confess we've given up." He nods. *"Oui,* it's your
efforts that have kept this war going for so long. Making
uniform after uniform with such love, melting down everything imaginable to make bullets, wearing nothing but home-
spun for years, managing the farms, and everything else. You
are truly Patriots in petticoats."

I'm speechless. He's given up years of his aristocratic life-
style to help our country, yet he is commending us Patriot
women for our devotion to the cause?

Raising his eyebrows, he winks. "All we men have to do is
fight when called upon by a superior officer." Amused by
himself, he chuckles and bends forward in a sweeping bow. "It
is with great pleasure that I shall inform General Washington
of your uncommon bravery."

I cut in. "No, General. I am so honored, but please don't
tell him. That's my only request of you, sir."

Lafayette stares at me, confused. *"Mais pourquoi pas?* Why
ever not? I don't understand."

"Sir, many others have contributed so much more,

including you. This is not about glory for myself, but glory for America."

He nods, stroking his chin. "If that is what you prefer, *ma chère mademoiselle,* then I shall oblige you, *bien sûr.*" He tips his tricorne hat toward me. "If nothing else, I am a man of my word. Later this morning I shall dispatch James to offer his services to Cornwallis. Then *voilà,* he can guide them here. He certainly knows the route." General Lafayette snickers. "However, thanks to your bravery, Cornwallis shall receive a crushing disappointment. May God speed you on your return. *Bon courage!*"

As much as I want to linger for days, I don't have another second to spare; I must leave immediately. In a few short hours, the inevitable sunrise will come. The Redcoat bugler will sound reveille, rousing the sea of troops blanketing our plantation for morning roll. Then hundreds upon hundreds of Regulars will be alert to observe my suspicious return. There is no safe place to hide right now, not until I'm snug in Mother's bed. Alas, even that's a mere illusion.

My heart sinks as I turn to Stith. I hate to leave him so soon; we've barely had a chance to talk. I haven't even gone yet, and I already miss him. Alas, I have no choice. I must make my way back to Bollingbrook.

As I'm about to hug him, I brush up against a thick bandage on his right forearm. I gasp. "Stith! What happened? I didn't know you were injured!"

He gives me a nonchalant smile and waves me off. "No worries, Sukey, I got off far easier than most. It was just a silly musket ball, and the surgeon got it out with no infection."

Relieved, I embrace him with what little strength I have left in my aching arms, savoring each second. Finally I step back and wipe my cheeks. "Now I must return to Mother, lest those hateful Redcoats discover my absence and punish her for it."

Stith's droopy eyes are misty too. "Indeed, you must. Once the area is clear, I'll try to circle around to the Petersburg depot and visit Bollingbrook on my way back to Guilford Courthouse. I have to know you're all safe. I'll be thinking of nothing else until then." A look of pain flashes across his face. "I feel horrid leaving you and Mother undefended, but I'm so proud of you both. You are far braver than me. Farewell, Sukey girl."

CHAPTER 23
LOST!

Mounting Raven once again, I close my eyes and brace myself for the inevitable pain. Indeed my weary, chafed thighs all but groan in agony, and my long legs cramp up. Muscles ache all over my body, many of them entirely new to me. I seek inspiration, asking the spirit of my great-grandmother Pocahontas to guide me home.

There is a loud rustling straight ahead. Suddenly in the shimmering moonlight, a massive buck with a towering rack of antlers bursts out of the woods. Then he bounds across the trail, and a petrified Raven bolts in the opposite direction, almost rolling me off. I lean forward, wrapping my hands around his neck, and hang on with every shred of strength left in my body. With reckless abandon he thrashes in circles, changing direction so many times I lose count.

I'm stunned. Within a scant few minutes, I no longer have any idea where I am and even less of an idea where the trail is. I am lost. Yes, I have Father's compass, but even the best compass can't direct me to the narrow road. Heading in the right direction is far from enough. Raven and I certainly can't navigate our way around miles of trees and dense brush and still make it home before dawn. For such a complicated situation, the outcome is all quite simple really. If I can't find my way back to the trail soon, I am finished.

Even though I finally manage to bring Raven to a stop, rolling waves of dizziness wash over me. My body has never felt so detached from my mind. Despite my heaving chest and racing heart, I can only take in short gasps. With a tingling sensation running down my spine, I'm on the verge of full panic. My instinct is to flee, but there's nowhere to run but further into the shroud of darkness, making my situation even direr.

Somehow I have to summon the inner strength to calm down. Otherwise, my fear of impending doom will come to fruition right here. Closing my eyes, I press a trembling hand to my chest, willing it to slow down. Eventually I'm able to take a full breath. As I regain my wits, I swat at the mosquitos feasting on me and scratch their itchy, raised bites.

After a slow dismount from Raven, I rest my forehead on his heaving side and then feed him an apple. I'm ready to make a bargain. Although I'm ashamed to admit it, even to myself, my intentions haven't always been noble. Desire for glory has motivated my every daydream. However, I'm now resolute.

"Raven, you are my witness. If I can make it back to Bollingbrook, I shan't boast of this, not to anyone, ever." My mission is now about America triumphing, not my individual quest for greatness.

With a sigh, I walk him through the brush to prevent stiffness, not caring as burrs attach themselves to Stith's clothing. "Here, Raven, I'll let you guide us. Unfortunately I've no idea anymore." I let the reins go slack and traipse alongside him, my heart heavy.

After a few minutes of aimless wandering, he comes to a

halt and paws at the ground. Thankfully the invisible sea of chirping crickets and croaking frogs cuts through the eerie stillness of the night.

"Yes, I know, Raven. I'm anxious to get going too. But how are we ever going to find the trail?" However, I give a start when he nickers and stomps on the ground. Good heavens, it's the sound of hard-packed dirt! As I pull some branches aside, the moon highlights a spectacular sight. Raven is standing right on the trail's shoulder. He's found our lifeline! Suddenly I'm about to cry tears of joy.

Although my heart is swollen with gratitude, I have an unpleasant realization. I'm still quite disoriented. In fact, I have no idea which direction to take. Within seconds, though, Father's compass remedies the problem, and we are back en route. However, now a new worry plagues me. I have no idea how much time passed while we were lost in the brush. In my state of anxiety, it seemed like hours. Surely the sun will start to rise soon, which will mean doomsday for me.

At long last, I approach the barn back at the Blands' and am anxious to dismount. However, in the darkness I land on a jagged rock and stumble, triggering more shooting pain in my injured ankle. With a decided limp, I walk Raven behind the barn. Looping the reins around a tree, I take a precious moment and lay my head on his mane, not caring that it's lathered up with perspiration.

"Dear Raven, I must hide you or the British will surely take you. I'm so sorry to leave you after all you've done for me, but the sun will rise soon!" I hesitate. Of course, I'm not sure when that will be. "Not taking off your saddle after riding all night, shame on me! I'll do it anyway, heaven help me!" I unfasten the straps as quickly as I can, fumbling to remove his heavy saddle and the drenched pad underneath. "Oh, Raven, doesn't that feel good?" The horse whinnies and shakes his mane, showering me with warm droplets of sweat. I am too worn out to shield myself or even wince.

"Now I must go. Once the British have passed, I'll bring you back to the barn. I promise." I peck his nose and pat his steaming flank one last time. "Thank you, you've been brilliant." Grabbing the lantern, I head toward the river, stumbling along with my bowlegged limp. Despite several mishaps, my mission has been successful so far, but it's far from complete. Many things can still go wrong, and time is running out.

CHAPTER 24
STRANDED

Gritting my teeth to offset the excruciating pain in my throbbing ankle, I scurry down the shadowy path, hoping my luck will hold out a little bit longer. With my lantern aloft, I scan the area for my canoe, but I don't see it anywhere. I'm bewildered. Then with each passing second, panic rises in my throat like I'm slowly drowning. Is it gone? But how did it disappear? Where did it go? Perhaps I didn't pull it up far enough, and the current swept it away. Maybe a British scout discovered it. But it doesn't matter why; it's gone.

Without my canoe, I must swim. I want to sink onto the riverbank and sob, but I haven't the time. I've never been quite so tired, even when Mary and her baby expired as the sun rose two fateful years ago. With my whole body hurting, I doubt my stamina to make it across, let alone the energy to hoist myself up onto the dock should I make it that far. But once again, I have no option. I allow myself the luxury of taking a deep breath, even more grateful to Mother I'm not wearing my gown and bulky petticoat. I kick off my shoes.

Then after a moment's hesitation, I blow out my lantern and put it down, the hardest step of all.

As I enter the water up to my knees, I'm overcome with thirst. Scooping a handful of water, I drink it in and look back to shore one last time, my heart full of longing. And then I spot the dim outline of my canoe! Relief floods through my veins like I've downed a jigger of brandy. Slipping my shoes back on, I limp over to the canoe and pull it toward the river. After several tugs, I've finally got it there.

Now wading in the water again, I dread the act of stepping into the canoe. No matter how I do it, I will have to put pressure on my aching ankle, an agonizing thought. After a moment of resolve, though, I lead with it. Wincing, I draw in the other as fast as I can.

I release a deep exhale. At long last, I'm back in my familiar canoe again. "Almost home, almost home," I whisper, pushing the paddle against the riverbed with all the feeble strength I can muster. After several thrusts, I enter into the current, and my spirits rise. Soon my strokes create a soothing rhythm. Despite my overwhelming fatigue, I welcome the delicate breeze on my warm cheeks as I drink in the river's musky scent. I savor my tranquil surroundings, knowing it won't last much longer. As I expected, though, making my way against the swift current is torture for my sapped muscles. With patience I didn't know I possessed, I gently slide my paddle into the river and pull it through the water over and over again, alternating sides.

Thanks be to God, I was able to warn General Lafayette, but my neck remains at stake, not to mention those of Mother, our slaves, and Bollingbrook itself. That durn Cornwallis! If he hadn't burned the tents, then I'd have more cover making my way back home. If just one Regular observes me, the consequences will be horrific.

As I pass the neighboring plantations, I hope our friends

are enduring this lobsterback invasion as well as can be expected, even Betsy. As much as she sets my every last nerve on edge, I certainly don't wish ill upon her.

Finally, after a long stretch of quiet exertion comes a most delightful sound: water sloshing up against something hard. Huzzah! I must be approaching the dock! All of a sudden my home casts a dark shadow on the already blackened river. I take a few more strokes and pause to assess the distance. I can't afford to miss it; I have to make it on my first try. No matter how careful I am, turning the canoe for a second attempt would cause some noisy splashing. Of course, I mustn't ram into the dock with a horrific boom either.

After a last tentative stroke, I scramble to the bow, keeping my weight low. Then I lean forward with my arms outstretched. If I've judged it right, I should be able to grab hold of the dock in seconds. At long last I'll be back home! The thought makes me want to weep, but I must focus.

But no, no! With my mouth hanging ajar, I realize my canoe will miss the dock, just inches beyond my extended reach. Desperate to bridge the gap, I lean even further out; now only my knees remain in the canoe. As adrenaline pulsates through my tingling body, I'm resigned to plunging into the river if I must.

Much to my surprise, though, two hands reach out from the dock and grab mine in a rough grip. With a gasp, I lock eyes with the crouching figure pulling me in. It's all over now; I've been discovered.

CHAPTER 25
CAUGHT AT THE DOCK

My body is numb, and I'm afraid to breathe. Oh, the irony of it all! I delivered the message to General Lafayette and made it all the way back, only for a filthy Redcoat to catch me at my own dock.

A small man and I stare at each other, but I can't see him in the darkness. Finally, he stammers, "Miss Sukey?" His voice sounds oddly familiar.

Summoning my courage, I whisper, "Who are you?" The Lobsters certainly don't know my nickname, save for Thomas Frederick. Although he's the roving overnight sentry, this man certainly isn't Thomas.

He presses closer, speaking in the faintest of whispers. "It's Leroy."

I gasp, not sure if I heard him correctly. "Who? Leroy? No! Is it really you?"

Although the darkness obstructs his face, he nods. "Yes'm, it's me, the slave who done run off, the first one ever." He hangs his head.

I hesitate. Should I trust him? After all, I no longer have any power over him. With a mere shout, he could report my suspicious arrival. Regardless, though, I must get out of my canoe; I'm far too vulnerable here. As I shift forward, he offers me his hand. With my muscles on the verge of failing, I have no choice but to reach out and grab it. With measured movements, I crawl onto the deck as he helps me forward, gently pulling my shoulders.

Still on his knees, he leans into me, whispering, "Miss Sukey, I got something to tell you."

Without thinking, I flinch and pull back. Now I'm close enough to see his eyes widen.

"Miss Sukey, I ain't going to hurt you none. No, ma'am!" He shakes his head double-time.

"I've got something to tell you, too, but let's get inside the tunnel first. Come, Leroy." He obliges me with a grunt as I shoo him in and pull the door shut. "Now, let's find ourselves a lantern." I need all my wits about me should I have to defend myself if he becomes ornery.

As we fumble in the darkness, Leroy's rank body odor bombards me. Thankfully he declares, "I got one right here, Miss Sukey." There is the sound of steel striking against flint. Thanks be to God, it sparks on the first try. Within seconds the lantern is aglow. This is all so bizarre. If it weren't for my desperate circumstances and Leroy's outlandish mishmash of rags and gaunt appearance, we could be any young mistress and her slave boy.

I turn to face him. "Leroy, you gave me such a fright out there! I could've sworn I saw you marching in here yesterday, but I wasn't sure. I didn't dare say a word to Penny. She's been so worried about you."

Leroy shifts his stance and looks down at the dirt floor. "Yes'm, you was right. You done seen me. And I done seen you and my sister standing there, so I got as far away as I could."

I don't understand, but there's no time to probe. "But why were you out there on the dock?"

"Miss Sukey, I never been so tired in my whole life, but I couldn't sleep none, not a lick. Mighty strange being here again, so I set myself on the bluff to get some air." He pauses. "I done saw you paddle off and knew you got to come back sometime before morning."

I'm incredulous. "So you waited all night for me? Out there on the dock?"

He meets my eye, nodding with a sheepish smile.

"Well, aren't you going to turn me in, Leroy?"

With a shrug, he hangs his head again. "No, ma'am. I don't want no trouble for y'all."

I can't make any sense of it. "Why not?" He has no reason to keep mum, especially after how Mother and I treated him. Surely he'd enjoy some vengeance against us. After all, catching a spy certainly would boost his stature in the British Army.

"We moving out this morning, don't know where." After a pause, he raises his head and looks me in the eye again. "I don't want to go with them. I done made a big mistake leaving here."

I'm baffled. "But why?" My mind is racing; I want to barrage him with questions. "You've wanted to join the Redcoats for a long time. I even heard you tell Big Hank!"

"Them Redcoats say we going to be free. But I don't believe that talk, not no more. We got to walk at the end, stealing food for everybody else. Ain't nothing ever left for us. Oh, I'm so hungry and so tired." He tears up, and his jaw tightens. "And if you get the pox, they leave you right there, no chow, no water, nothing, and they gone."

I'm flummoxed; I don't know what to say.

Suddenly the cellar door flies open. Spreading his arms

wide, Leroy pushes me behind him and hisses, "I got you, Miss Sukey!"

Penny stands in the doorway, dumfounded. "Leroy! Stop! What you be doing to Miss Sukey?"

I move up next to Leroy. "Hush, Penny, everything's all right. He was just trying to protect me. He helped me land at the dock. Otherwise I would've passed right by it."

Open-mouthed, Penny stares at Leroy and then back at me.

Leroy stares at the ground again. "I may as well just say it. I want to stay, but nobody here want me none."

I respond, "Mother would be happy to have you back, Leroy."

Penny raises her brows, doubt enshrouding her face.

"Really?" His eyes light up but then narrow. "How you so sure?"

"Well, she owes you an apology." I pause. "We all do."

He stares at me, slack-jawed. "But why? For what?"

"It's about that missing jewelry."

Leroy's chest swells. "Miss Sukey, I'm telling you again, I didn't take nothing." His voice rises. "Nobody ever believed me none, not even my own sister." He glares at Penny as she presses her lips together and looks down at the ground.

"Well, I'm so sorry it took us so long, Leroy, but we believe you now."

He breaks into a broad smile. "Why you change your mind?"

"Well, Penny doesn't know this either. But last night before I left, Mother and I found both pieces." I swallow, continuing sheepishly. "They were on the floor behind her bureau, covered in dust." I'm disgusted with myself. Why didn't we think to look there long ago?

His head moves forward as his eyes bug out. "You ain't joshing me?"

Penny bursts into tears. "Oh, Leroy." Her voice breaks. "I'm so sorry. You were right all along, and I wasn't believing you. I been a terrible sister."

"I must go see Mother now. Stay down here, both of you. I'll come get you after Cornwallis is gone." I scamper up the stairs to Mother's room, ignoring my shaking thighs. Much to my relief, I go undetected. To my great joy, I find Mother huddled on top of her bed, still clad in her same gown. Her haggard eyes brim with tears as she rushes to me. "Sukey, I never stopped praying for you all night long."

We cling to each other, both weeping. I have so much to say, yet I'm unable to speak through my tears. Her warm embrace is divine; I never want it to end.

Eventually she pulls back and murmurs, "How are you, my dear child?" Still holding my arms, she takes a look at me. "Oh dear, look at that nasty bruise on your forehead and all those scrapes! Now let's get you out of those muddy rags at once!" With deft fingers, she gently unties my tattered bonnet and lifts my chin, cupping it in her hand, which warms my heart. I've never felt quite so cherished.

I am dying to unleash a torrent of animated whispers to fill her in on my odyssey. But I can only blurt in a raspy voice, "I made it; I found him and told him!" Before I can get any further, though, a fist pounds on the door. Mother and I both jump, and I am struck with terror. Perhaps someone did observe me returning after all! And even if not, I must hide fast! No one can see me like this. Why, I must look like such a fright with my bloodied face and disheveled hair, not to mention Stith's oversized and torn clothing! Despite my pants still being soaked to my knees, I jump into the bed with my shoes still on and pull the blankets to my hairline and pretend I'm fast asleep. Mother smooths down her wrinkled gown and adjusts the pins in her collapsing bun. With a beleaguered sigh, she pulls open the door.

"Good day, Lady Bolling." My heart pounds as I stifle a gasp. Why, it's General Cornwallis himself! Much to my relief, though, he is in high spirits, not like he's about to apprehend a dangerous spy. "Alas, I would like to inform you of our imminent departure. We shall set off on a noteworthy mission today, but nothing for you to concern yourself." He chortles. "I don't make a practice of bothering a lady's head with military strategy and certainly don't want to wake your daughter. However, once our mission proves a success, I do intend to celebrate with a long, restful sleep such as hers." He chuckles, amusing himself to no end.

Holding my breath, I listen as Mother feigns agreement. "Certainly, General. Keeping this plantation profitable requires all my energy. I can't handle any more than that."

General Cornwallis continues. "Madam, you have provided us with utmost hospitality as you promised on our arrival. Since you've kept your end of the bargain, I shall so keep mine. Unlike General Arnold, I am a man of my word. To oblige you, we shall leave Bollingbrook as we found it."

Of course, I am elated, but irritated as well. Bollingbrook is certainly not the same place as when they descended upon us. Among many other acts of destruction, he failed to acknowledge that his army consumed our every morsel, trampled our new crop of tobacco, and destroyed our fencing.

"Also, due to our dwindling supplies, your slaves shall remain here. We haven't anything to feed them, let alone the thousands who've already joined us."

Hallelujah! I repress the urge to shriek with joy. Penny, Big Hank, Auntie Ruth, and all the other slaves are safe!

"However, I must warn you. This plantation shall soon become the King's spoils of war. After that, only time will reveal his plans for it." He chuckles. "Perhaps he will award it to a worthy officer such as myself."

I don't have to see Mother to know she is using every bit of energy to hold back a fierce scowl.

When she closes the door, I still have so much to tell her, but sleep has blissfully taken possession of my bone-weary body. Alas, I am too tired to dream or even hear the buglers play their reveille.

Soon after Cornwallis finally departs, Mother shakes me by the shoulders until I awake. In my woozy state, I'm baffled. It takes me a moment to remember why I'm lying in her bed besieged with so many aches and pains, as well as such intense hunger and thirst. Once I remember, the terror on her face jars me.

"What is it, Mother? What's happened?"

"I hate to wake you, Sukey, but Penny... She's gone! Those horrible brutes have taken her with them after all." She breaks down in sobs. "We can't find her anywhere!"

My heart goes out to Mother. "Oh, Mother, she's here, she's safe. She's down in the tunnel with Leroy."

Mother jerks her head up, and her jaw hangs open. "Leroy? Leroy's here? At Bollingbrook?"

"Yes, yes, he is! He saved me at the dock when I was about to pass it. He wants to come back home."

"Of course! In fact, I insist. I have amends to make, and there are so many chores for him in here, especially now."

CHAPTER 26
AN ARTICLE AND A LETTER

LAFAYETTE THWARTS KIDNAPPING ATTEMPT BY
CORNWALLIS
THE VIRGINIA GAZETTE

S*tymied by the relentless sabotage of supply lines by the North Carolina Patriots, Lieutenant General Charles Cornwallis recently defied the strict orders of the Commanding General Henry Clinton. Without notice, he abandoned his secure foothold and moved the entire British Southern Army to City Point, Virginia. Then he attempted a surprise capture of Major General Lafayette just ten miles north at the Half Way House in Richmond.*

However, thanks to a tip from an unidentified Patriot informant, Lafayette thwarted this nefarious plot with ease. The same spy also informed Lafayette of Cornwallis's plans to set up a permanent camp near Chesapeake Bay to receive supplies and send troops to assist in the defense of New York City. As a result, our beloved Lafayette is currently employing his masterful skirmish-and-retreat tactics, leading Cornwallis on a merry game of chase throughout inland Virginia. Bravo, Lafayette!

20 October 1781

Dear Sister and Mother,

Oh, Sukey girl, it was so brilliant to see you, even if for a few weary minutes in the wee hours. I've often wondered if I dreamed it. But no! It's hard to believe that was almost three months ago. Thankfully, Lafayette's assistant James got word to me that you made it back to Bollingbrook in one piece. My heart ached to stop there on my way back to Guilford Courthouse, but Lafayette thought it best to avoid the area should Cornwallis circle back after you thwarted him. Yes, you! You thwarted him! Brilliant work!

We immediately moved north to Virginia to support Lafayette. Oh, what an outstanding General he is! He played quite a game of cat-and-mouse with Cornwallis, leading him all over Virginia. Finally in August, the weakened Cornwallis rested in Yorktown's deep-water port to await transport back to New York against our impending attack, or so those foolish Lobsters believed! Oh, little did he know what was in store! How I wish you could hear me cackling here alone in my tent.

Our resounding victory in Yorktown yesterday was all due to Lafayette's vision. And that is no exaggeration on my part. Back in August, he noticed that Cornwallis hadn't bothered to build any fortifications and developed a grand scheme to trap him there. General Washington also proved himself a master of deception once again; our cunning Fox. Although he changed course on trying to recapture New York, he left our encampments there fully staged. Then he drafted false plans in his own script and arranged for a convenient British interception.

Come early September, the French fleet defeated the British Royal Navy off the Virginia Capes, blocking Cornwallis from the water. General Washington and French Commander-in-Chief Rochambeau stealthily marched their armies over 550 miles, arriving late in the month. Huzzah! At last, we had Cornwallis trapped, and then we constantly bombarded them. With supplies depleted and the pox running rampant, Cornwallis cast thousands of his trusting runaway slaves out of camp. A great number died, but we captured many and will return them to their owners. So much for the Redcoats' guarantee of freedom!

Yesterday they finally conceded the battle while their band played a melancholy rendition of "The World Turned Upside Down." Huzzah! Never have I been prouder to be an American! Naturally the cowardly Cornwallis feigned illness and sent O'Hara limping in his stead to represent him. Even worse, O'Hara attempted to offer his sword of surrender to the French General Rochambeau. You'll be happy to know Rochambeau just shook his head and pointed over to Washington. This humiliating defeat certainly revealed their true character, which doesn't surprise me any.

What parties there were here last night! The Redcoat officers were there as well, with one notable exception. Tarleton! The Butcher feared for his safety since we Americans despise him so much. His absence probably saved his life, but it would have been such good fun to see him torn apart, limb by limb.

My heart bursts with pride to be your brother, even more so than usual. You see, you are the real hero behind our victory. This is no exaggeration, Sukey! Without you saving Lafayette at the Half Way House, Yorktown never would've happened. Rumors have been flying around about a young lady who warned Lafayette and saved our cause from extinction. A few even asked me if I knew her identity, yet I shrugged and said nothing. I will keep your secret to my grave if that's what you wish, my Sukey girl. Rest assured, though, I'm confident that someday the world will know you as the Girl Who Won the Revolutionary War.

Your brother and son,
Stith

EPILOGUE

As Stith explained, Lafayette successfully evades Cornwallis at the Half Way House thanks to Susanna's warning. Then Tarleton heads to Monticello to capture Governor Jefferson, followed by members of the General Assembly in Charlottesville. However, Patriot soldier Jack Jouett overhears their plan. He rides through forty miles of back roads to warn Jefferson. Jefferson barely escapes by hiding on nearby Carter's Mountain in the hollow of a tree. Tarleton captures several legislators and destroys nearly 400 barrels of gunpowder and 1,000 new muskets. Meanwhile, Cornwallis and his troops stay at Jefferson's breeding farm, Elkhill, and destroy it.

Soon thereafter, Peter Francisco volunteers to spy on Tarleton. When Tarleton's men surround him, he kills three dragoons and escapes with their horses. He keeps one for himself, naming it Tarleton.

James Armistead serves as Cornwallis's waiter during the Yorktown Campaign, relaying crucial intelligence that leads to the miraculous American victory. However, after the war, James remains enslaved because he is considered a spy, not a soldier. Bolstered by a testimonial from Lafayette, he lobbies the General Assembly and gains his freedom. He takes Lafayette as his last name and goes on to own slaves himself.

The General Assembly drops all charges against Governor Jefferson. He goes on to serve as Secretary of State under President John Adams and the third President of the United States.

The two fingers that Tarleton lost at the Battle of Guilford Courthouse prove to be an asset for his political career. He is elected to the House of Commons for over twenty years. Likewise, General Cornwallis is treated like conquering hero upon his return to England. King George III appoints him Governor-General of India and later Ireland.

Peter Francisco teaches himself to read and write. During his last years, he serves as the Sergeant-at-Arms for the Virginia Assembly. During the American Bicentennial, the US Post Office issues a Peter Francisco stamp, honoring him as "Fighter Extraordinary" and "Contributor to the Cause." Four states celebrate Peter Francisco Day on March 15.

General Lafayette participates in the French Revolution of 1789, earning the nickname of "Hero of Two Worlds." He sends a key to the Bastille to his dear friend, George Washington, now on display at Mount Vernon, and also names his son Georges Washington Lafayette. He spends seven years in an Austrian jail for being anti-monarchist.

In 1824, President James Monroe invites Lafayette to visit America where he receives a hero's reception. For over a year, he tours all twenty-four states, refusing to turn down a single dinner invitation. While touring Virginia, escorted by Peter Francisco, Lafayette spots James Armistead Lafayette in the crowd, stops his carriage, and rushes to embrace him.

During France's July Revolution of 1830, Lafayette declines an offer to become dictator. At his request, he is buried in Paris with soil from Bunker Hill. During World War

I, the first American troops who arrive in France march directly to Lafayette's grave and announce, "Lafayette, we are here." In 2002, Congress makes Lafayette an honorary US citizen. Over 150 places in the US are named for him.

Young William Henry Harrison of Berkeley Plantation does indeed grow up to a military hero in the Battle of Tippecanoe and a Major General in the War of 1812. He holds various offices until serving as the 9th President of the United States in 1841 but died soon thereafter of pneumonia.

AFTERWORD

This story of Susanna Bolling is based in truth, and I thank you for reading her story. Until now her heroism has been little more than a footnote in obscure history books. This novel was written with as much historical accuracy as possible, supplemented with details from the time period.

However, for ease of reading, I made several small changes. First, Susanna's home was actually called Mitchell's. However, for the purposes of this book, I referred to it as Bollingbrook Plantation, which belonged to close relatives.

Second, Susanna actually had three brothers, including her oldest Robert who served with great bravery in the Continental Navy. In the book I reversed the names of her brothers Stith and Alexander because Stith is such a memorable family name.

Third, Susanna was technically not related by blood to Pocahontas. Susanna's ancestor, Colonel Robert Bolling, married Pocahontas' granddaughter, Jane Rolfe, who had children but later died. This line of descendants is referred to as the "Red Bollings." Susanna comes from the following union of Colonel Robert Bolling and his SECOND wife, Anne Stith. They are referred to as the "White Bollings."

ACKNOWLEDGMENTS

It has been such an honor to bring Susanna's amazing true story to life. In the process, I have learned so much about the American Revolution and the prominent role that women played in it. Thank you, Petticoat Patriots, for your many sacrifices and unsung contributions. America is forever indebted to you.

Thank you to my incredible husband Bernie, for your unwavering encouragement, support, and generosity in reading draft after draft. It is no exaggeration to say that I couldn't have done this without you. You are definitely my better half.

I am so grateful to Kristen-Paige Madonia, Sheena Billett, and Alison Jack for their fantastic editing which has made this a much better book. Also a huge shout-out to Dane at Ebook Launch for the absolutely fabulous cover.

Heartfelt thanks to my many early readers, especially Cynthia Abalos, Jayda Justus, Mary Helen Sheriff, and Colleen Lee who slogged through multiple drafts with such thought-fulness.

As for my research, I am especially grateful to the Virginia Museum of History & Culture and the Library of Virginia for their amazing resources. Also many thanks to the Historic Petersburg and Battersea Foundations for their hospitality and Melanie Woodford of the Royal North Carolina Regiment for her spinning expertise.

I am indebted to SCBWI and James River Writers for the countless conferences that helped me develop my craft as a writer, as well as the incredible support from the amazing writer network in Richmond.

A gargantuan thank you to Steven K. Smith for helping me navigate the bewildering world of publishing, as well as Ali Plautz, Scott Stavrou, and Lane Orzak.

And to the many cheerleaders who kept me (somewhat) sane throughout the process, especially Alston, LoLo, Dede, Cathy, Lynne/SIL, and Mom – thank you! To my amazing Georgetown '88 buddies, couldn't love you more!

Last but certainly not least, a special shout-out to Mary at the Little Bookshop, Rick and Sue Young at the Half Way House, Jane McCullen and the Historic Hopewell Foundation, Stefan Calos, Greg McQuade at WTVR CBS-6, Martha Burton at Petersburg Area Regional Tourism, and all who have so generously helped me promote this book.

Please look for "Susanna's Midnight Ride" at George Washington's Mount Vernon, Jefferson's Monticello, the American Revolution Museum in Yorktown, St. John's Church, the

Boston Tea Party Ships Museum, the Valentine Museum, Chop Suey Books, Blandford Cemetery, Sweet Dixie, and Weston Plantation.

Lastly, I am so thankful to Greg Meyer for telling me Susanna's story and then encouraging me to share it with the world. Thank you, Joy Meyer, for bringing us together.

ABOUT THE AUTHOR

A writer and lawyer, Libby McNamee loves exploring America's many historical sites. When a descendant told her about Susanna Bolling's heroism, Libby was determined to share it with the world. Susanna's Midnight Ride is her first published novel.

Libby served as a US Army JAG Officer in Korea, Bosnia, Germany, and Washington State. She and her book-obsessed husband and son live in Richmond, Virginia. A Boston native, Libby graduated from Georgetown University *cum laude* and Catholic University Law School. Check out her blog, "Libby With a Y" at www.LibbyMcNamee.com and drop her a line at Libby@SagebrushPublishing.com.

facebook.com/LibbyMcNameeAuthor

twitter.com/LibbyMcNamee

instagram.com/LibbyMcNamee

WANTED

READER REVIEWS

Online reviews are so helpful for indie authors like me. They help spread the word and give our books more credibility. If you could take a few minutes and give an honest review at any of the websites below, I'd be grateful.

AMAZON.COM
GOODREADS.COM
BARNESANDNOBLE.COM

Thank you so much!

Libby

Made in the USA
Monee, IL
13 December 2021